To
Christof

CODE NAME
BLOODY
WINTER

From
Me ma

CODE NAME
BLOODY WINTER

ROGER ELWOOD

WORD PUBLISHING
Dallas·London·Vancouver·Melbourne

Library of Congress Cataloging-in-Publication Data

Elwood, Roger.
    Code name: Bloody Winter / Roger Elwood.
       p. cm.—(The OSS chronicles)
    ISBN 0–8499–3387–0
    1. World War, 1939–1945—Fiction.   I. Title.
II. Series: Elwood, Roger.   OSS Chronicles.
PS3555.L85D4 1993
813'.54—dc20   93–11024
                                                     CIP

34569 LBM 9 8 7 6 5 4 3 2 1

To Brady Smith—
Fellow traveler

Author's Note:

Code Name: Bloody Winter is the third novel of the OSS Chronicles series. We are coming to the end of the World War II segment and soon will be entering a post-war period when the OSS, for which Stephen Bartlett has been working under the direction of William Casey, was renamed the CIA.

Wolf's Lair and *Deadly Sanction,* the two previous titles in this series, were laced with innumerable and quite solid historical facts and this present entry is hardly less so. As *Code Name: Bloody Winter* delineates, before war was ever declared, Hitler had started to organize the most massive penetration in history of an enemy country by espionage agents.

From 1937 through 1945, nearly a hundred—some sources place the figure at more than a hundred—men and women came to the United States and entered the fabric of American life with no attendant suspicions, for they seemed quite ordinary and notably unsinister.

But what they were doing was planting bombs, some of which remain undetected and unexploded even today, poisoning water supplies, copying secret governmental and industrial documents, assassinating anyone who happened to be standing in their way, and blackmailing corporate executives and even members of Congress as well as key Pentagon employees.

Interestingly enough, it was not the first time that a militant German government brought the covert dimension of warfare to the continental United States. Saboteurs carried out a remarkably similar series of actions during World War I. According to records in the National Archives and the Library of Congress, the undercover network set in place by Germany committed nearly two hundred acts of sabotage prior to America's entry into the war in 1917.

Ironically, this had proved to be a major miscalculation by the German military and intelligence communities. The resulting backlash from Americans and their representatives in Washington, D.C., changed from a course that favored nonintervention into one that entailed full-bore involvement that consequently brought Germany's defeat and humiliation.

Yet today, fifty years later, the average American has no idea that any of these activities happened at a time when it was assumed that the United States was an impregnable fortress, its troops soon to be disgorged on foreign battlefields of Europe and the Far East.

Part One

1

It couldn't have been the food.

At a certain restaurant just under two miles from the Capitol building in Washington, D.C., any possibility of bad beef or chicken or some other dish seemed to have been virtually eliminated through a list of safeguards that was part wartime precaution (since so many lawmakers, military men, and undercover agents were known to eat there and as such, it could become a target for saboteurs) and equal part the tradition of quality that had been pursued by the conscientious owners for decades.

Curiously, though, people were starting to feel ill.

A senator from the Midwest was the first to complain. He was followed by a prominent four-star general and then a long-time special aide to the president of the United States. Yet the nausea for the three of them passed quickly enough, and the staff's panic subsided, everybody expressing considerable relief.

Someone, a celebrated mayor from one of the New England states, stood up, smiling, as he proposed an eloquent toast to the seven guests at his large round table in one corner of the restaurant.

"May the Nazis beg us on their knees for mercy!" he said quite jubilantly, the other diners (not only the ones in his party but also those who overheard him) joining in and repeating a statement with which no one had trouble agreeing.

And so it went that evening, loud toasts and boisterous conversation alongside quiet little dinner meetings between two or three individuals, with the sound of an old-fashioned player piano in the background.

The mahogany-paneled walls of that renowned spot had been witness to endless numbers of whispered secrets and displays of public boasting and wild indulgence as well as quiet romance ever since the end of World War I, when the restaurant was built and immediately became a hit with the bureaucratic crowd as well as foreign visitors who wanted to be seen where the power centers of that city were dining. Nearly thirty years later it had lost none of its mystique.

At about ten o'clock, a number of diners started to leave, more than a few of them drunk, since all had heard the most recent good news of how the war was going, and they wanted to let off steam after a long and depressing period of bad reports from the various battle fronts.

Quite a few lived nearby and had decided to walk to their homes, the chill October air feeling good against their cheeks, now hot with intoxicating alcohol. They left their assistants and aides to take care of the government cars.

Most never made it. The powerful men died in the arms of their crying wives or mistresses or girlfriends, joined in death minutes later by the women themselves, their bodies sprawled from one end of the neighborhood to the other.

But it was back at the restaurant that the worst scenes were occurring, dozens of people screaming as their insides knotted up and pain gripped them from head to foot. Some died in an instant, their hearts overwhelmed by whatever had caused the trauma to their systems. Others gasped for breath as though plastic bags had been yanked over their heads, suffocating them.

In a desperate bid for fresh air that was nonexistent in the smoke-filled interior, one member of the Armed Services Committee jumped through the front window and died an instant after he hit the concrete sidewalk, glass shards embedded in his face, one of them a long, knifelike piece that missed his left eyeball but had made it into his brain.

Washington police and various FBI and OSS agents reached the restaurant in just under twenty minutes,

Stephen Bartlett was one of them.

The colonial-style restaurant, its facade freshly painted white, was located on a short and narrow side street that led off Pennsylvania Avenue. Clusters of official state department cars, police vehicles, ambulances, and fire trucks as well as the private cars of those who lived or worked or visited in that area quickly clogged it. The overflow spilled out onto the main thoroughfare all the way to the gates of the White House, where President Franklin Delano Roosevelt and his wife, Eleanor, worried about some staff members whom they knew had planned to eat dinner in that particular restaurant.

On the adjacent sidewalk and across the street from the restaurant was a growing throng of chattering men and women, some with the appropriate agencies but others drawn out of curiosity. They mingled with reporters and photographers, who were no more sensible in those days than in later years when moments of crisis arose, offended if someone felt it more important to attend to those in pain rather than answer their questions or pose for a fast photograph.

Stephen Bartlett was accompanied by William Casey. Veteran Federal Bureau of Investigation Director J. Edgar Hoover joined them a short while later, which seemed unusual since it was hardly his normal *modus operandi* to go directly to the scene. In general, he preferred to run the bureau strictly from the confines of his office at headquarters, where he had the protection he felt he deserved.

But this was different, a deadly attack just two miles from the Capitol building, and not much farther to the White House. It seemed as though the Nazis were pointing obscenely at the Americans and asserting their superior skills in such activities.

"So many!" Hoover exclaimed, his normally ruddy complexion suddenly pale and white. "I know most of these people. Some very good friends planned to be here tonight to celebrate something or other."

"All of them dead . . . or dying." Casey spoke, also profoundly shaken by the disaster that he was witnessing. "I feel for you; I feel for you deeply."

Hoover nodded, appreciating the words of sympathy.

"I'm going inside," Bartlett muttered, not content to wait around any longer.

"You don't think there's another shoe to fall, do you, Stephen?" Casey asked, knowing that his top agent didn't do *anything* rashly.

Bartlett shrugged his shoulders, then hurried across the street and entered the restaurant, now illuminated imperfectly by moonlight, its murky interior filled with broken glass, overturned tables, chairs with legs askew, dishes and their contents scattered in every direction—and numerous puddles of blood.

He stood quietly in the center of the semicircular main room, getting a feel for the surroundings. All around him, patrons were being carried outside by medics and others. Some of them were dead; a few gasped in pain, the rest "merely" unconscious.

Bartlett recognized a few of the men, normally powerful figures eager to flaunt their influence, now abruptly reduced to the state of whimpering, helpless babies foaming disgusting greenish fluids from their mouths, unable to stand or walk, leaning on other men to whom they normally would have paid no attention at all, wrapped up as they were in the cocoons their political positions had constructed for them.

Government of the people, by the people, and for the people, Bartlett thought cynically. *Where has it all gone?*

One of the medics who had just come in from the street recognized him.

"Stephen!" he exclaimed. "What a mess! Any ideas, buddy?"

"None so far," Bartlett replied, recognizing the other man as Art Linson, a tall, broad-shouldered, dark-haired, high school football chum.

He inhaled, letting out his breath slowly.

"Smell anything?" Bartlett asked.

"Not really," Linson told him. "What's going on?"

"Gasoline maybe?"

"I don't—"

The other man cut himself off, testing the air.

"You might be right," he admitted, a tense expression on his face.

"But where's it coming from?" Bartlett asked cryptically.

"Up there maybe, Stephen," Linson said as he pointed to one of the air vents in the plaster ceiling.

Bartlett nodded, then grabbed a chair and stood on it as he stretched up to examine the vent more closely.

"Probably some leaking air pump or—," he mused outloud.

Noises.

He heard noises coming from beyond the vent.

At least two voices, in harried tones that betrayed their nervousness, speaking about what they had been filtering into the restaurant.

And suddenly Bartlett knew.

"Art," he said, as he jumped off the chair, "we have to clear everyone else out of this place, get them as far away as possible."

"Why? What did you find?"

"No time. Help me, please. I'll take care of the guys in here. You tell the others outside. Get them as far away as you can."

Linson nodded, then left.

One by one, Bartlett approached the other medics who lingered inside, telling them to hurry. Two protested, but when he flashed his OSS identification, they flushed with embarrassment and started to file out.

"*Now!*" Bartlett screamed to the remaining handful, his gaze darting for an instant to that grill in the ceiling. "*Run for it!*"

He had made it to the pavement and halfway into the street when the interior of the restaurant abruptly was set ablaze at the same time it was wracked by an explosion.

An ambulance directly in front of the restaurant was sent several feet in the air, landing amidst the crowd of onlookers. Various other vehicles were knocked on their sides or jammed against others with such force that windows shattered and hoods were flung off and sent flying dangerously. A motorcycle flew upward with such force that it tore the front entrance to a two-story executive apartment building off its hinges and landed on the marble floor of the foyer. More than one gas tank burst open, creating trails of the noxious liquid from one end of that small side street to the other.

Hoover, normally a man able to rein in his emotions, showed signs of panic, although he tried to cloak this under the guise of concern for the three of them.

"We must hurry!" he said excitedly. "Those scum responsible for this would be very pleased if they got all of us as a special bonus."

They joined the crowd that was racing toward Pennsylvania Avenue to escape what proved to be a growing holocaust, set off by the explosion inside the restaurant. Someone was muttering, "Yea though I walk through the valley of the shadow of death, I shall fear no evil: for thou are with me."

Hoover saw that it was an old woman.

"May we help you, ma'am?" he asked in a kindly manner.

"Sasha and I were out for a walk," she mumbled, her eyes dazed-looking. "He became so terrified that he broke away from me and ran up the street. I don't know what has happened to the poor little thing."

Hoover put one arm around her.

"Will you join me?" he suggested.

"Aren't you—?" she spoke, studying him.

"Yes, yes, I am," he replied. "But, please, for now, we really must hurry along. Is that all right, dear lady?"

She smiled slightly and started to walk with him. Casey and Bartlett followed just behind them.

Suddenly there was a second explosion precipitating bursts of flame from within and around the restaurant; great masses of fire spit forth as though from some mythical dragon transported somehow to the reality of the nation's capital.

Fire seemed to be chasing the fleeing customers and onlookers, catching up with the slower members of that crowd. Their cries of pain filled the air, making that scene similar to one that might have come from Dante's *Inferno*.

One man was suddenly covered with a shroud of orange-red flame. Casey and Bartlett heard his agonized screams and turned for a moment, transfixed. The body fell dead less than a foot in front of them, and they had to jump back to avoid contact before running again.

Yet another explosion was the most violent of the three. It blew off the roof of the restaurant building, scattering shingles in every direction, some of the pieces landing blocks away, and shaking the ground under them with such force that Hoover, who suffered from a never-publicized congenital balance problem much like Meniérè's syndrome, fell to his knees, his face shiny with perspiration.

For a moment the FBI director did not speak, disoriented by the loss of balance he was experiencing.

"Help me!" he muttered unnecessarily, despising the impression of weakness that this created but suddenly feeling very ill.

Bartlett grabbed one arm and Casey took the other, and they assisted him the few remaining feet to Pennsylvania Avenue. The old lady whom Hoover had befriended took hold of his hand, and was rubbing it gently, glad to have the opportunity to return his display of kindness.

"I feel so weak," he was mumbling. "It's awful to be seen like this."

"You're being human, my dear," she spoke softly. "Is that so bad? When push comes to shove, you are like other men, you know."

He looked at her, smiled weakly, and tried to fight the nausea that threatened to get rid of the contents of an early-evening dinner at another restaurant.

Pausing for breath, Bartlett momentarily examined the crowd that was surging in every direction. He noticed several more senators running in terror, followed by an assistant to the secretary of defense.

This city is supposed to be insulated from the war, protected by security measures, he thought. Over the years, it has also become detached from the nation its officials are supposed to be serving. No one is prepared for cataclysms of any sort.

The rampant panic he saw in virtually everyone in that area was what made three other men stand out. His attention focused on them as they walked a little too nonchalantly from that side street until they reached the main thoroughfare. One was quite short, the other two of medium height.

No fear.

He saw no fear written on their faces, contorting their features. Instead they seemed to have a body rhythm that bordered on arrogance.

One of them turned, saw him, and then looked quickly away.

Then the man and the others turned down a street two blocks over, their shadows betraying the fact that they all had started running.

"Those guys!" Bartlett muttered urgently to Casey. "They're not acting at all in a normal manner."

"Panic, Stephen," the OSS director told him. "*Nobody* is going to be behave normally, whatever that means, in a situation like this."

Bartlett had earned the freedom to cut through protocol and disagree openly with William Casey, not a typical position for anyone working with the man.

"But why only them? I can't accept their behavior as fitting in. There's something wrong about them."

"I don't know," Casey admitted. "You haven't seen how *everybody* is behaving. Let's forget three guys and concentrate on—"

Bartlett interrupted him, something even he seldom dared to do.

"I have a hunch," he persisted. "Those guys seemed to be headed in the direction of the German Embassy."

"As you know, that's been closed down for a couple of years. It's checked over whenever possible. No activity has been detected there in a long time, Stephen."

Bartlett's expression was convincingly skeptical.

"All right," Casey told him, chuckling a bit at what was hardly unaccustomed tenacity on the other man's part. "Go ahead. But don't take unnecessary risks. Is that clear?"

Hoover had been following their conversation.

"Stephen . . . ," he said, his voice weaker than usual. "I'll have some agents assigned and sent out right away. But they won't approach you unless they suspect trouble or you give them an actual signal."

Bartlett thanked him, glad that Hoover hadn't demanded an all-out assault, undoubtedly a normal response in such a situation, for that could have been embarrassing if his hunch failed to pan out, or it could have meant much carnage should the suspected Nazis be prepared to battle it out in the wake of what had happened at the restaurant, realizing that they had little to lose under the circumstances.

He set off behind the three men, careful to maintain enough distance between them and himself so that they wouldn't suspect that they were being followed.

The trio stopped for a few minutes at a two-story office building, where a short, gray-bearded man opened the front door. They talked for a few seconds, each gesturing excitedly, and then went on their way.

Probably a Nazi front company housed there, Bartlett thought as he noted the address and the appearance of the man who had greeted them so that an armed FBI team could be sent back in the morning.

As he continued following the three men, he thought of all that he had been able to learn about the various clandestine Nazi espionage rings operating inside the United States.

During the prewar years, the United States had been what one source described as "a spy's paradise," with a vast underground that reached up into nearly every defense contractor and branch of the military establishment as well as even the federal government itself. Naval and army officers were kidnapped, others bribed, and various Americans privy to military secrets were tortured into revealing what they knew.

All this had happened because, unprepared for the coming battles, the federal government imposed few restrictions, not realizing how shortsighted this attitude was—a kind of innocence fostered in part by Nazi sympathizers operating at various levels of the bureaucracy, eager to give their soulmates as much free rein as possible.

CODE NAME: BLOODY WINTER

We had no agency assigned the task of dealing with such activities, Bartlett recalled. *There was no viable military intelligence branch, and the State Department's counter-subversive force consisted of one man!*

He remembered what had happened as far back as 1929 when the U. S. Signal Corps came very close to deciphering topnotch foreign codes. Henry L. Stimson, who was then secretary of state, flatly rejected the special measures being advocated by the USSC's best men. His reason was offered without equivocation: "Gentlemen simply do not open other people's mail."

"It's nothing less than astonishing!" he had been told by William Casey just after the two of them and their respective families had taken off from Heathrow Airport. "Those devils have scores of undercover agents from coast to coast. For every thirty or forty we manage to round up, we can be certain that at least an equal number remain."

"But how do they get in?" Bartlett asked. "Don't the Customs and Immigration Departments keep a tight lid on things?"

"Impossible!" Casey pointed out. "Many are natural-born citizens who have harbored secret allegiances to National Socialism. How do we separate them from the others, men and women who actually abhor what is happening in Germany? We cannot treat *everyone* the way Roosevelt has insisted we treat the Japanese. One crime like that is enough!"

Casey then tried unsuccessfully to conceal a certain amount of admiration for the man behind the monumental Nazi espionage rings.

"When Wilhelm Canaris was imprisoned as a traitor, the Nazis' undercover activities lost the advantage of being the brain children of meticulous planning," he went on. "The German spy system not only was left without the guiding genius who had made it what it was, but this came about because Canaris had decided to turn against the *Führer* and plot with von Tresckow, Beck, and the others for a new regime that would end the war and allow the Allies to be victorious . . . a humiliating time for spies sponsored by the Fatherland! To be honest, I am surprised that the admiral's not been executed before now.

"Lahausen, a subordinate, remarked that Canaris had human qualities that placed him far above the usual military bureaucrat. This made him decidedly a hated figure among the cold, cynical monsters surrounding him. Though they all admired his abilities, in retrospect

19

they thought his apparent ruthlessness during the earlier years to be somewhat suspect, a clever guise to hide his true nature."

Casey was uncharacteristically shivering.

"Is there something else?" Bartlett asked.

"There is *always* something else," came the weary reply. "We have found out that the Nazis have at their disposal the *Mikropunkt.*"

"What in the world is that?"

"It was developed in Dresden, a process that permits them to photograph any sheet of paper they wish, however large, and reduce it to no more than a postage stamp. Once the original shot is taken, we can assume hurriedly, they transfer the film to a revolutionary new microscope that further shrinks it so that, ultimately, it is no bigger than this."

He had taken out a sheet of paper from an inside pocket of his business suit and used a pencil to put a dot on it.

"It can be hidden anywhere," Casey added. "Once back in, say, Berlin, all these little dots can be blown up to the size of a wall, if they wish!"

"Virtually undetectable . . ," Bartlett said. "A student could be carrying a term paper, and all the periods could be instead tiny snapshots of defense secrets, for example."

"We would have to examine every sheet of paper in the possession of everyone entering or leaving the United States. An impossible job!"

"Our enemy has the ideal espionage device!"

The rest of the flight back to the States was spent mostly in silence.

Now, less than six months later, on treelined Massachusetts Avenue, Stephen Bartlett stood behind a thick-trunked tree across the street from the German Embassy, which had been filled with suspicious activity and individuals until its forced closing, the familiar old brick building a dismal-looking place in the best of times.

The three men he followed from the nightmare scene outside the restaurant had ducked around the back.

Surveillance of the embassy had become rather minimal in recent months, due to valuable manpower resources' being kept busy tracking down tips about Nazi espionage targets in the United States, particularly President Roosevelt.

"We must get this devil!" an intercepted communiqué had stated. "If he dies, we can work with the isolationists in Congress and cripple the war effort, even at this late stage. *Roosevelt must die!*"

CODE NAME: BLOODY WINTER

The National Socialists had long harbored a special loathing for FDR, since the president of the United States had defeated the influence of the often Nazi-backed isolationists. As a result, he incurred some political damage initially, but this later turned to admiration and support from the largest possible majority of the American people. As soon as the U.S. forces entered the war, the *Führer* saw his hopes vanish for an unbroken series of quick victories, and even he could understand that it was no longer a foregone conclusion that Germany would win.

Hitler had held only contempt for Neville Chamberlain, rightly thinking him to be vacillating and weak, an unworthy opponent. In contrast, when Winston Churchill became prime minister of England, the list of hated and implicitly feared adversaries grew by one. But there was no serious consideration given to assassinating either of the others. If anything, the Nazi high command hoped to capture Churchill and de Gaulle and parade them before the world as the ultimate human trophies. Only Roosevelt provoked the kind of venomous response that drove Hitler to the fury he usually reserved for the *Juden* of Germany and the rest of Europe.

Some evidence had been turned up that the Japanese high command had a part in the plan to "get" Roosevelt. They knew he hated them because the bombing of Pearl Harbor had happened on his watch. But there was more to it than that. They were aware of his treatment of Japanese-Americans, treatment that even Roosevelt's supporters found far too harsh.

So FDR became a special target of potential assassination attempts funded by both the Nazis and the Japanese!

FBI agents uncovered the fact that master spy Fritz Duquesne, one of the most dangerous Nazis alive in those days, had picked FDR's Hyde Park, New York, residence as a possible location for an attack, so the president avoided going there for the remainder of the war.

At the same time, it was learned that other Nazi targets included the White House itself and the few remaining locations where the president could be expected to appear, causing the Secret Service to intensify the protective ring around the entire presidential family.

They knew we would be unprepared for anything like that restaurant being hit, Bartlett thought. *It always seemed far more valuable as a place for overhearing potentially useful snippets of conversation. Blowing it up makes no sense.*

Unless . . .

The very idea made him sweat from head to foot.

Unless the Nazis had emerged from their collective delusion to realize finally that the war was going badly for them and that they must do anything they could to cripple the United States, on the battlefield *and* at home, on its very soil.

After looking from side to side, Bartlett quickly crossed the street and walked down the same narrow alleyway that the three saboteurs had just used, careful not to bump into any trash cans or other objects.

A stale, unpleasant odor hung in the air, the kind found in abandoned buildings as they fell into disrepair, becoming the hangouts for depression-spawned drifters and other bums whom the war-generated recovery had left untouched.

Initially, along the front half of the former embassy, Bartlett had detected no lights inside as he glanced through one window, then another.

And then toward the rear—

A gas-filled lantern partially illuminated the faces of the three men and a fourth figure, a woman.

He recognized her!

The woman was Paulette Brisbane, one of the more active Washington whores, someone who had become well known to the FBI and the OSS for her sexual activities, but apparently nobody had suspected her of going so far as to commit espionage.

The window, which reached halfway to the ground, was open less than an inch. Bartlett listened carefully.

"You must get this to Rolf immediately," one of the men was saying in German. "He will know what to do with it. As for us, we have to go back into hiding."

He handed the woman a sheet of paper.

"How many?" she asked.

"Dozens, Fraülein Brisbane," he told her. "A very good catch."

"Was it necessary to do what you did?" she asked sharply.

"We had to kill the man. He was an important link that had to be broken. We decided to do so without any indication that he alone was the target. This was accomplished. His death was but one of many. None of the Americans will suspect."

"Too much chaos too early in the game," the woman protested sternly. "Your actions may backfire and cause more trouble than they solved."

"We simply had no alternative. Besides, you know as well as we do what is supposed to be in full operation next week. The Americans will never be able to discern the difference, thinking this act is somehow connected with the other."

"But, Hans, do you not realize that we have given them that very week to act on whatever suspicions are generated?"

Her anger was apparent as well as her contempt for their actions. She reached out abruptly and slapped the one man hard on his left cheek.

"Fool!" she said, nearly shouting. "Stupid, bloody fool!"

Bartlett was reaching for his Colt .38 revolver when a hand clamped down on his shoulder. He forced back a startled cry as he swung around.

"Stephen! Thank God I caught you!"

Fellow OSS agent Mark Lunsford, who was every bit as tall and rugged-looking as Bartlett, stood, grim-faced, just behind him, motioning him away.

"Follow me!" he whispered. "It's important."

When they were across the street and out of hearing range, Lunsford said, "I'll take your place, pal. Casey wants you right away. Something incredibly urgent is on the table. And you're the star agent these days. He wouldn't settle for anyone else."

Lunsford spoke out of admiration rather than jealousy.

"A car's waiting a block east of here. The rest is already taken care of. Half a dozen other agents will be on the spot in minutes. We'll trap those guys inside before they can destroy anything helpful to us. Bet on it. Casey's back at headquarters, firmly in charge of the command center."

"But I just left him. He's supposed to be with Hoover."

"He was, but a couple of minutes after you headed off in this direction, we got a report from someone at the agency.

Lunsford frowned as he added, "This is a lot bigger than any of us could have imagined, Stephen."

"A major sabotage offensive?"

"Right on the money. The restaurant is but one of dozens of targets."

. . . You know as well as we do what is supposed to be in full operation next week. The Americans will never be able to discern the difference, thinking the one is connected with the other.

Bartlett told the other man what he had heard.

"There might be a connection, as you say," Lunsford agreed.

"But all I know for sure is that Casey happens to be planning for Armageddon to rain down upon us at any moment, and he is convinced Hoover will support him without argument. Which, you have to admit, would be a big change of pace for the old bulldog!"

"Is all this supposed to be happening clear across the country?"

"Apparently, and everything's being so well planned that it makes the rest of us look almost like wet-behind-the-ears amateurs, I'm afraid."

Bartlett shook his hand and started to leave.

"Stephen?" Lunsford spoke.

"What is it?"

"The Nazis have a special code name for the operation, and they are assigning dozens of agents to it."

Lunsford gulped as he added, "They've called it . . . *Bloody Winter.* Doesn't that tell you everything? *We're in for a winter of pure hell, pal.* It's going to be—"

Across the street . . .

They could hear a door slamming shut, as though it had slipped out of someone's grip, and some low voices, cursing.

The three men were leaving.

"We can't wait," Bartlett said. "Look! They might be setting other bombs in place tonight while there is still so much chaos in the city."

Relenting, Lunsford nodded in agreement.

"Let's get them now!" he whispered.

The three had started to cross the street to the other side, though cautiously so, ready to run if necessary.

Guns cocked, Bartlett and Lunsford jumped into the center of the cobblestoned street less than a dozen yards from them.

"Freeze!" Bartlett told them. "Federal agents!"

At the end of that block, a high school bus had suddenly come into view as it started to turn the corner, its headlights distracting Bartlett and his partner for a moment. An important football game had been played earlier in the evening, and the teenagers on the bus were ecstatic over their team's victory.

The middle spy, by far the shortest of the three, turned and waved his arms in front of the bus, forcing the driver to brake quickly. The other two drew their own handguns and started shooting.

Bartlett and Lunsford fell to their stomachs and returned the fire. One man was hit in the chest and doubled over. The other turned and ran up to the bus, joining his fellow undercover agent as they pushed open the door and jumped inside.

The driver was jerked out of his seat, and the shorter man took over behind the wheel, slamming his foot down on the gas pedal.

Bartlett and Lunsford hesitated, thinking they could get the driver, but knowing the bus would then be out of control, endangering the lives of its innocent passengers.

So instead of firing, they tried to jump out of the way, but Lunsford wasn't fast enough. He was hit by the right front fender. The bus barreled down the street and headed up another toward the main thoroughfare out of Washington.

"My arm! My ribs!" Lunsford cried out after he was slammed against the thick trunk of the same tree they had been hiding behind seconds before. "Stephen . . . I think they're broken!"

His face was contorted with pain.

"Don't wait for me, Stephen!" he pleaded. "I'll be all right. Go after them! They've got all those kids!"

"Where's that car you mentioned?" Bartlett asked.

His question was answered a split second later as a dark green Oldsmobile appeared from off an intersecting street and stopped just to their right.

Two agents jumped out and started to hurry over to them.

Neither made it.

Deadly bursts fired from a machine gun brought both down.

"Where the h—?" Lunsford gasped.

They could see nothing at first. There were no streetlights nearby and the moonlight was filtered out by trees branches that hung like an archway over both sides of the dark street.

"There!" Bartlett said. "She's—"

The Washington whore.

Stepping out of the shadows only a few yards away, she was smiling as she now aimed the weapon at them and shouted, "Death to the *Juden* lovers! Heil Hit—"

Her attention was diverted by one of the agents she had shot groaned as he groped for his pistol.

She swung the machine gun quickly toward him, giving Bartlett a chance to aim his pistol and pull the trigger. His first shot caught her in the left shoulder, the second missed altogether. For a moment she struggled to keep her grip on the much heavier weapon but couldn't. She dropped it.

In that instant she seemed to be quite helpless. Bartlett felt a very real temptation to fire directly into her chest.

It would have been *easy* for him to do just that.

He and Lunsford would be more than able to come up with some story about what had happened.

"Fall down on the asphalt!" he yelled at her instead, "and clasp your hands your back. Now!"

The pain that had been spread over her face changed into a leer, followed by laughter, hoarse and chilling.

"I'm going to turn and flee," she spoke, her voice surprisingly deep. "You *won't* shoot an unarmed *woman* in the back! I know that much about your kind."

She did what she said she would do, but Bartlett didn't. She wasn't able to take even a single step up the street and away from him before he aimed and fired two rounds.

She looked stunned as she fell.

"You're right about your back. No gentleman would *ever* shoot you there, but that doesn't include your legs!" Bartlett shouted with some pleasure. "Now, it seems, you're going exactly nowhere."

He turned his attention to Lunsford and saw that he was still conscious. Then he rushed over to the two other agents, bending down beside them.

One was dead, the other still alive.

"Is your radio functioning?" he asked.

The survivor nodded. Then abruptly his eyes widened and he tried to say something while raising one arm and trying frantically to point.

Bartlett turned around and saw the woman inches from his feet. She had pulled herself along the street to get to him.

Raising herself as far as her knees, she swung at him what she had managed to conceal until then, a small knife, grazing the back of his right hand. He had reholstered his pistol and was forced to scramble for it while she hit him again with the blade, this time making contact with his neck and gouging out a sliver of skin.

He rammed his hands under her torso, lifted her up, and threw her back and away from him. She tried to stand but her legs were useless.

Bartlett could see an expression of pure evil on her face.

Suddenly the woman looked at the knife a bit numbly and tossed it to one side. Reaching into a side pocket of her dark maroon overcoat, she pulled out a crumpled folder of matches and struggled angrily to open it.

Bartlett noticed a familiar odor.

The tank of the agents' car had been hit minutes earlier. Little streams of gasoline were trickling from it in several directions. "For the greater glory of *Deutschland!*" the woman shouted in a grotesque display of triumph as she struck one of the matches and, after it ignited, tossed it onto the street. She immediately started to light another.

The bullet from Bartlett's Colt got her in the middle of her neck. She clamped both hands reflexively just under her chin and gurgled several times as she fell forward into a widening puddle of blood and gasoline.

As the first match had touched one of the little streams of liquid, it burst into flame, spreading in rapid succession to others.

Thinking quickly, Bartlett saw that Lunsford was well away from the flames. He turned to the other agent, still crumpled nearby. "Go!" the agent yelled to Bartlett. "Get out of here. You can't make it if you have to drag me along with you!"

Bartlett ignored the other man's plea, grabbing him under his arms.

Fire was now consuming the woman. It had also reached the agent's shoes, the heels and sides of which had become coated with gasoline.

"My feet! My feet!" he screamed.

In an instant his trouser legs were aflame.

Bartlett ripped off the ancient and by now shabby overcoat he had been wearing ever since he started with the OSS, an uncustomary personal gift from William Casey, and threw it over the man's body, but by this time, the gasoline had spread to the rest of his clothes and he was rapidly being engulfed.

Screaming wildly, the agent broke away from Bartlett. He rolled over once, twice, three times, trying to stop the consuming flames, but disoriented and in agony, he succeeded only in placing himself next to the car itself, right in the center of the leaking gasoline.

Then, barely conscious and not knowing what he was doing, he reached out for its front bumper and pulled himself up before abruptly shaking his head as a rampaging spasm of intense pain tore through every inch of him, and he dropped back onto the cobblestoned street, his body twitching violently before it went limp against the crackling, spitting sounds of rapidly spreading flames.

2

Within less than five minutes, two carloads of heavily armed FBI agents had arrived, followed by a fire truck that had been shifted temporarily from the restaurant scene half a mile away. Yet another fire in the midst of Washington, D.C. could not be allowed to spread to any additional buildings.

Stephen Bartlett told one of the agents that he wanted to go after the school bus and would need a car.

"*We* can handle it," was the curt response from that pale-looking individual whose body language suggested hostility.

"What is your name?" Bartlett demanded, having no difficulty detecting the other man's animosity.

"It's Christopher Lyons. And don't bother introducing yourself. I *know* who you are. Some at the bureau are foolish enough to admire you, but I don't. You're a grandstander, Bartlett. You get the big assignments and use them to your own advantage. Everybody else works hard in your shadow and gets ignored."

Sarcasm was etched on his face.

"Besides, this isn't OSS's jurisdiction," he growled defiantly. "Let me suggest that you get the h—"

Bartlett smiled broadly.

"I don't see what you find so funny," growled Lyons, who was five feet ten inches tall and much thinner than Bartlett, and whether admitting it to himself or not, he was intimidated by the considerable bulk of someone he loathed.

"You should stop while you are ahead," Bartlett urged as he glanced past the other man and noticed the individual who was getting out of the black sedan that had just pulled up across the street from them.

Lyons's manner remained unchanged, his body language projecting his defiance.

"Get out of the way, Bartlett," he spoke coldly.

"Don't say I didn't warn you," Bartlett added.

Lyons was about to say something else when a long-familiar voice stopped him cold, and his face blanched.

"Are you having any difficulty, Stephen?" J. Edgar Hoover asked as he approached the two of them.

"We were just getting ready to leave, sir," Bartlett assured him, privately enjoying Lyons's readily apparent embarrassment.

"Going after the school bus, I assume?"

"Yes sir."

Hoover's expression was serious, dark circles heightened by what had been happening in the course of just an hour.

"You're in charge of this matter, Stephen. I know that isn't normal procedure, but these are hardly normal times. My men are to follow your orders as though I were present and giving them myself."

He took Bartlett by the arm and asked him to step to one side for a moment.

"Something's happening, Stephen," Hoover remarked in a whisper. "The Nazis are desperate by now, which is understandable, considering their fortunes on the battlefield. But I hate to think what they are up to because we all know what they are *capable of* since they have little or no conscience."

He looked up at Bartlett, who was a few inches taller.

"Stephen, I have some good men on my team," he added. "But I do envy Bill Casey. You are a remarkable individual. But then you don't like to take too much credit for what you've accomplished, do you?"

"No, sir, I don't. The credit for whatever I am, whatever I've done that has any worth at all, must be given to God. Without Him, well, I don't know where I would be right now or the kind of human being I would have become."

"There was a time when I might well have called you naive, Stephen. But your experiences have been so remarkable that there can be no other explanation. Casey has been kind enough to keep me informed over the past few years. Perhaps you and I could talk more privately one of these days."

"I would like that, sir."

The two men shook hands heartily.

Hoover turned to Christopher Lyons.

"You are to leave immediately," he ordered brusquely. "Whatever it takes, you've got to apprehend those lousy—"

He stopped himself, not wanting to curse in front of one of his men, especially since he had been solely responsible for a dictum against bad language.

Seconds after Hoover had left, Lyons turned to him, a worried look on his face. "I was out of line, Bartlett. I apologize."

He extended his hand.

"I'm sorry you feel the way you do about me," Bartlett replied, shaking it. "I'm going to tell you what happened to my family and me earlier this year. I think you might want to change your mind after I finish."

He quickly described to Lyons the attack against their isolated house in the English countryside, the kidnapping of his wife and son, and then himself, his loved ones' ordeal at Dachau, and the numerous other moments that had brought them close to death.

Lyons was about to react with some shock when another agent came running up to the two of them.

"Jersey!" he announced breathlessly. "We got a tip—I have no idea where it came from—but they say the bus is heading for New Jersey. Maryland troopers spotted it, but it keeps switching roads. It's going to be difficult to keep up."

Lyons snapped his fingers.

"I wonder if they're headed toward the pine barrens!" he exclaimed. "I've long suspected that that whole area is ideal for espionage and who knows what else—many square miles of nothing but trees and a few hillbilly types living away from everybody else."

He thanked the other agent.

"Get Connors and come with us, okay?" he spoke.

The agent nodded, and waved to another man.

Then the four of them jumped into the nearest of the two FBI cars, with Lyons driving and Bartlett beside him.

"Which route?" Lyons asked.

The agent answered with the directions that had been relayed to FBI headquarters.

"I was born near Atlantic City!" Lyons said as he floored the gas pedal, tires squealing. "I know that whole South Jersey area. *We're on the way!*"

"For the sake of every one of us who's a father, we *have* to get those guys!" Bartlett proclaimed, banging his hands down on the dashboard.

Patrick Connors, one of the two agents in the back seat, leaned forward and tapped Lyons on the shoulder.

"An airfield perhaps?" he offered.

"But that wouldn't be much help. We could blow them out of the sky."

"Not with those hostages," Bartlett reminded him. "I can't believe they're not going to take some of them along!"

Lyons was silent, feeling more like a rookie than someone who had been with the FBI for five years.

"It's difficult for me to get used to some swastika-loving foreigners *invading* this country to destroy us," he said after a bit. "It's like they're raping my wife or my daughter. I just want to get my hands on them and—"

Regaining control of himself, Lyons glanced at Bartlett and, through the rear-view mirror, at the two men in the backseat.

"Am I crazy or what?" he asked.

"I think we all feel pretty much the way you do," Bartlett assured him. "On that bus might be as many as half a dozen teenagers whose fathers and mothers would agree with you, Christopher."

That thought energized them as they tried very hard to catch up with a vehicle being controlled by men on orders from a regime that had already sacrificed the lives of millions in its maniacal quest for world domination.

Past midnight.

Forty-five minutes later they spotted the bus, which apparently had been stopped on a side road in a heavily wooded area and was backing up onto the highway at a speed that made its heavy old frame visibly shudder.

"After it!" Connors shouted. "Get the sons of b—"

"Wait!" Bartlett said. "Look!"

Bodies.

Four bodies on the dirt shoulder, their clothes torn, their limbs at various angles, two with their eyes still open, the pain of how they died frozen on their faces.

Lyons slammed on the brakes.

The four agents jumped out and raced to the bodies.

Three teenage boys and one girl.

"All dead!" Connors groaned. "I think they're—"

One was still breathing!

"He's just barely alive," Bartlett said as he felt the pulse of one of the boys, who was very broad and tall, undoubtedly a member of one of the football teams that had been playing that night.

Bartlett placed two hands gently under the young man's head and lifted him up an inch or two.

"We . . . we tried to overpower them," the words came slowly, with considerable pain, "but . . . but we weren't quick enough. They started shooting like madmen. And then they dumped us like we were sacks of garbage . . . just threw us out the door."

Bartlett wasn't surprised by that, after having seen what conditions were like for the hapless prisoners at Dachau.

"It's not you," he said. "It's the way they look at the rest of the world. If you're not with them, you can only be against them, and *that* makes you nothing but a candidate for immediate extermination."

The young man's eyes rolled up in their sockets.

"It hurts . . . ," he said. "It hurts worse . . . than anything . . . I think I'm going to die. Are . . . are the others okay? Jennie, is she—?"

"Ambulances are on the way," Bartlett told him, dodging a direct answer. "It won't be long now, son."

"Sir . . . I . . . I . . . think I know where they're . . . headed. I . . . I understand German. I just can't speak it."

"Where are they going? Tell me, son, if you can."

"In Jersey . . . near Vineland . . . they're . . . they're going . . . going . . . to . . ."

The young man coughed up some blood.

"So cold . . . ," he said.

Lyons was standing next to Bartlett now. He whipped off his coat and placed it over the teenager.

"An . . . airfield . . ."

Those were two of the last three words he said before he died. Abruptly he stopped groaning, and whispered, "Jesus . . ."

Then his body became limp against Bartlett's arms.

Lyons and Bartlett glanced at one another.

An airfield near Vineland, New Jersey.

"I have an idea, Bartlett," Lyons spoke. "We *have* to get to the saboteurs *before* they reach any plane that may be waiting. If they take the rest of those kids with them as their hostages, we've lost it all.

"As we agreed before, we can't just go and shoot a plane out of the sky. Even if, somehow, there aren't any hostages involved by that time, in the event that it does belong to a foreign power, one with which we are not at war, we'd still find ourselves unable to dispose of the saboteurs. We've got to apprehend them before then, whatever it takes."

"You're right," Bartlett agreed. "Getting them *after* they board any plane just won't cut it. Who knows how long it would take us to get permission? And where are they going to be by the time we finally do . . . *if* we did?"

"Probably in South America somewhere," Lyons suggested. "I'm personally betting on Argentina."

"Where they *love* Nazis!" Bartlett exclaimed. "The Argentinean government has been unofficially sending out word, in anticipation of a forthcoming debacle in Europe, that all National Socialists are assured of safe haven in that country. But, of course, they'd be happier if only the wealthier ones took them up on it."

"Goering and the other Nazis are greedily amassing great collections of art and hidden bank accounts and whatever else, even as Germans and Jews and Gypsies alike are dying all around them." Connors spat out the words, adding, "and in the process the entire German nation is going down the drain. But you know what? I bet it's true that that gang of devils is probably already planning their getaways!"

"If they don't commit suicide," Bartlett added sardonically. "Men like that will do anything to avoid being held accountable."

"One of us should stay here," Lyons commented, pointing to the students.

The fourth man volunteered.

Before they left, Christopher Lyons radioed back to headquarters for immediate help with the bodies.

There would be more of the dead to come as the search for the bus continued.

3

Motorcycles.

Half a dozen of them were strewn on either side of the highway, two bent virtually in half. One of the riders had just finished using his leather jacket to put out the flames that had blackened the once-shiny metal of his cycle.

Lyons stopped the car immediately, and he, Bartlett, and Connors jumped out, heading over to the cycles.

The riders were not teenagers. They were older, tougher, and very angry, forerunners of the Hell's Angels groups decades later.

All had escaped fatal injury.

But, leaning on a friend's shoulder, one had cupped his hands in front of his eyes, murmuring, "I've been blinded! I've been blinded!"

Two were limping. One was holding his head as though his neck had been badly whiplashed. Another had a blood-streaked forehead and cheek.

The sixth one, biggest of the group, with a scraggly red beard, told the three agents what had happened.

"We couldn't pull over in time!" he said, gesticulating. "I whipped out my gun as soon as I could, but they were out of range."

His wide, bearded face went red as the three agents showed their identification.

"There's a permit in the pack on my cycle," he added, "if you want to see it. I'm Phil Beroskin, and my name's on the paper."

"No need for that now," Bartlett reassured him. "We'll radio for an ambulance. Anything you can tell us?"

"They were crazy," the large, bearded one recalled. "They just didn't care. One of my guys jumped on the back of the bus and was starting to look inside, to survey the situation. One of those creeps rammed a rifle butt through the window and shattered it. Pieces got into his eyes."

"We would love to help you get those guys," another biker shouted. "Two of our cycles are workin'. We could join you. We're used to fights. We have them all the time. Need some extra muscle?"

Bartlett thanked him but declined the offer, adding that it would be far too dangerous for any civilians.

"I have a little brother the age of those kids in that bus," Beroskin said. "I would go crazy if anything happened to him."

Lyons radioed for another ambulance and then he and the other two agents were on their way again.

1:37 A.M.

A roadblock involving a dozen New Jersey State Police officers and seven patrol cars had finally been set up directly ahead of the school bus.

The bus driver slowed the vehicle, then stopped it altogether.

"Send every hostage out now!" the saboteurs were told over a loudspeaker.

Christopher Lyons, Stephen Bartlett, and Patrick Connors waited outside their car a few hundred feet behind the bus, their own weapons drawn.

"Look!" Bartlett pointed.

The door to the school bus had been opened and a teenage boy had stepped out but as soon as his feet hit the road, he was stopped by someone inside who had looped a rope over his head and now held it tight around his neck.

"Somebody's holding onto him," Bartlett said.

The motor was no longer idling.

"Listen! And look at the wheels!" Connors added. "The bus is moving again."

"They're going to ram the road block!" Lyons said, his voice nearly a shout. "If the cars aren't moved, that boy will be crushed to death."

Seeing this and knowing that they couldn't just open fire, the troopers had no choice but to scramble into their cars and start opening up the roadblock.

The bus driver chose not to wait.

The vehicle picked up speed, forcing the teenager to walk

faster, faster, faster, then run, his feet pounding the asphalt road as he struggled to keep up.

"How can he keep it up?" Lyons muttered. "How can he—?"

The teenage boy tripped, fell, tried to get up. But by then the momentum of the bus was too strong. He was being dragged by the neck, the remaining cars in the blockade only a hundred feet ahead.

One of the FBI's best marksmen, Lyons jumped up, aiming his Colt. He fired once, then again, trying somehow to hit the hand that held the end of the rope or, failing that, the rope itself.

Too late.

The bus hit three patrol cars head-on, flinging them to one side or the other, collapsing the frames of two of them. For a moment it swerved as though the driver was losing control, then steadied and continued on.

Bartlett, Lyons, and Connors ran up to the state police officers who had rushed over to the teenager and were gathered around him. One had dropped to the ground beside the boy.

"He's dead!" the officer told Bartlett. "I think his neck was broken."

"How could he have kept up as long as he did?" Bartlett asked.

The policeman's eyes were filling with tears.

"What a waste. What a blasted waste," he replied. "I've seen this kid's picture in the paper. He was one of the best runners in the Northeast. He would have been a candidate for the Olympics. He had such a chance. He would have made it just then, I think, if he hadn't tripped. He must have gotten a cramp in one leg. That's what it looked like to me."

"Are any of your vehicles still operational?" Bartlett asked as he showed the trooper his OSS identification.

"At least two are, sir."

Bartlett told him about the bikers.

"We'll see to it right away," the policeman promised. "But don't the three of you want some help?"

"Call ahead for another roadblock. But get the nearest National Guard post involved this time, not because you guys can't handle it, but they have the tanks that'll be necessary. Any problem with this? I don't have the authority to order you to do anything. I can only tell you what I think."

The officer nodded.

"What you're saying makes sense, sir," he agreed. "I guess you'll be right behind those crazies, then?"

"We will. They're Nazi spies, not just run-of-the-mill criminals. A lot more is involved than just what's happening now."

"Do it for the kid here," the officer said, looking at the dead teenager. "Do it for him, will you?"

"And some other kids we found back there. That's a promise."

In a tableau that had become tragically familiar, the state policeman drew his jacket over that young body on the asphalt then hurried over to the other men. There was a moment of discussion, all of them nodding, and then they turned, giving the three strangers thumbs up just before they cleared their cars from the highway.

4

At an hour when it could never have been expected, a hearse, followed by a stream of mourners' cars, tried to get onto the highway from a township road just after Bartlett and the other agents crossed over to New Jersey. They were less than a mile from the bus.

Despite the late hour, traffic flowed steadily around them, headlights piercing the night. Carefully, the agents closed the distance between their car and the bus.

Suddenly the bus driver swerved to the left, sideswiping an oncoming vehicle, the cars behind it piling into one another, some ramming into nearby trees, windows shattering, one of the passengers flung through onto the hood.

The hearse was tossed over on its side, causing a heavy, dark, rosewood coffin to be pushed out the back doors by the sharp motion, its seals splitting open and sending the contents sprawling onto the highway.

Suddenly the bus was braked.

"What are they *doing?*" spoke Lyons. "And what's a funeral procession doing on the road so late at night?"

"Stop the car," Bartlett shouted. "Now!"

Lyons did just that.

"Look!" Bartlett said, his mouth dropping open as he tried to cope with what he was seeing just ahead of him.

Someone inside the bus had started firing at the passing line of cars.

"They've lost their minds!" gasped Connors.

"It must be that those guys figure they can't be in worse trouble than they are now," Bartlett said, "so they're going to try to take as many Americans with them as they can, whatever the consequences."

People dashed out of their cars and ran frantically for cover among the tightened pack of old trees on that side of the highway.

A woman and her five-year-old boy, jarred from sleep into panic, couldn't run fast enough to escape the barrage. The child was hit and fell to the ground, his chest spurting blood. His mother screamed as she wrapped her arms around him and started to haul him off.

A white-haired middle-aged man about five feet eight inches tall, his face deeply lined, stumbled toward her. He leaned over, kissed the boy on the forehead, and reached out, closing the child's eyelids, his hand trembling. Then he spoke to the woman briefly.

A moment later another man, younger and taller, gently took the limp body from her.

Bartlett, Lyons, and Connors were out of the car and crouched down in the dirt shoulder on the opposite side of the road in the hope of catching the saboteurs by surprise. They edged up to the bus, waiting for clear shots at both men.

Then something happened that none of them could have foreseen.

Six men jumped out of four of the cars in the procession. One was armed with a sawed-off shotgun, another with a Winchester self-loading ten-shot-magazine .351 rifle. The others had various pistols!

They aimed at the bus and started firing.

"Look!" Connors yelled, panting a bit. "They're deliberately not hitting the passengers' compartment."

The tires!

The six were shooting out the tires, along with the headlights, and then rendering the motor an inoperable tangle of severed wires, torn rubber hoses, and twisted metal. White steam came from its pierced radiator with an ominous hiss.

Other men were now streaming out of the cars, each with a handgun or a rifle or both. Two had Thompson .45 caliber machine guns.

"They've got the latest issue," Lyons said, noticing that the Tommys, long identified with the FBI itself, had the newer, easier-to-load, box-type magazine instead of the drum variety, which had been phased out after 1935.

Suddenly windows on the right side of the bus were shattered outward.

Two teenage boys and a girl were being forced up to the empty window frames. Terror washed their faces white in the darkened bus.

"We get a car or they *all* die!" one of the two kidnappers shouted, his accent almost a caricature.

To emphasize his point, he shot the girl in the head and threw her contemptuously to one side.

"No!" Connors, enraged, jumped up from the dirt shoulder and started to race toward the bus, his pistol drawn.

Bartlett tried to grab him and pull him back but failed.

"Don't do it!" he shouted. "You'll be caught in the middle."

One of the saboteurs swung around, saw Connors, smashed out another window, and started firing. The FBI agent was hit in his left side, the bullet splintering a rib. As he fell, he managed to get off one shot that blew away part of the other man's right ear.

But the man didn't drop his weapon. He continued to hold it with one hand while he grabbed a white handkerchief from an inside pocket of his overcoat and pressed it to what was left of his ear.

In the background, several teenagers screamed in terror until they were ordered to shut up.

"Put your guns on the ground," that same heavily accented voice demanded coldly of the men outside.

They glanced at the white-haired figure who was now standing off to one side.

"I'm not going to wait," the voice demanded. *"Drop them now!"*

At that the figure solemnly nodded, and the men deposited their weapons in a common pile at their feet.

"Step back!" the saboteur added. "Do it!"

They obeyed.

Bartlett could see the white-haired man, who was obviously the boss of the others, turn for a moment toward Lyons and himself and subtly shake his head.

"He *knows* we're here!" Lyons exclaimed. "Hey, doesn't he look like—?"

Lyons squinted, trying to see the man better in the semi-darkness created by the moonlight.

Bartlett was studying the man.

"Are you thinking the same thing I am?" he remarked.

"It *does* look like Santapaola," Lyons acknowledged. "Is that who you had in mind?"

Benedetto Vincenzo Santapaola, one of Al Capone's most prominent successors east of the Mississippi!

By accident, the saboteurs had run up against one of the few men, outside certain officials in the U.S. government, that they had every reason to fear, someone for whom rules and laws meant little. The additional irony was that Santapaola had arranged the late-night burial to avoid being spotted in the daytime by either the feds or a rival mafioso family. Friction between the various groups had been starting up again, despite the long calm imposed by Lucky Luciano and Meyer Lanski.

"Doesn't he realize we're federal agents?" Lyons asked. "He seems to have given us some kind of signal."

"I think I know exactly what he has in mind," Bartlett told them, his facial muscles tight, expressionless.

"What is it?" asked Lyons.

"At this point, Santapaola, I suspect, wants us to do nothing."

"I'm not hearing you right, am I?"

He waited for Bartlett to say something.

"Surely you can't be serious! That's the one thing we could never allow. And why would we take orders from a godfather who's nothing more than a murderer himself? You're crazy if you think—"

"Look!" Bartlett interrupted. "That's why we can't go racing out there like Connors did."

The teenagers were being led single file out of the bus, a saboteur on each side.

One of the two snapped his fingers and pointed at the nearest car, which had barely escaped being involved in the pileup. It was no more than a dozen feet away.

"That one!" he shouted at Santapaola. "You dago swine! Somebody bring the keys here! *Now!*"

Bartlett leaned over to Lyons and whispered, "Now tell me who you think is crazy?"

One of Santapaola's men stepped forward, dangling the keys from his fingers.

"Over here, ginnie trash!" the saboteur ordered.

The man winced at that but walked forward.

"Hand them to me!" he demanded.

As soon as the saboteur had grabbed the set of keys, he whipped the barrel of the pistol he was holding directly across the other man's lower jaw, dropping him to his knees as he cried out in pain.

"My name is Walter Schmidt," the gunman shouted arrogantly at the others. "It isn't Marinelli or Giovanni or gutter filth like that.

You creeps are not worthy to clean Nazi toilets! When the triumphant Deutschland rules the world, you will be treated like what you are . . . dung under the feet of your Aryan masters!"

The man he had struck reached, unnoticed, down to his right leg, edged up the trouser, and pulled a knife from a sleeve strapped just above the ankle. In one quick motion, he rammed the long, narrow, sharply honed blade of hard metal into Schmidt's side, then stood and ripped upward with it, his fingers clinched tightly around the handle.

The teenagers saw this and started running toward the trees where the terrified motorists were still gathered.

As the remaining saboteur swung his rifle up and was about to pull the trigger, one of the teenagers, a young man six feet three inches tall and weighing nearly 250 pounds, turned and dove for him, knocking him off his feet.

"Fool!" the gunman shouted as he managed to slam the rifle's barrel across the teenager's forehead, dropping him to the ground.

Pushing the boy's heavy body to one side, he stood, swaggering but only for a moment, hearing the familiar and unmistakable sound of firing mechanisms being cocked, one after the other. He turned slowly toward the sound.

Half a dozen weapons were now aimed at him.

He started to back away, toward the bus; then, without warning, he lifted the rifle and pulled the trigger. He got off only that one shot, which missed, before the six men poured the contents of their guns into him, wasting only a few bullets.

He fell against the side of the bus, then slid to the ground.

Benedetto Vincenzo Santapaola took a pistol from one of his men and started to walk slowly up to Schmidt, who was not quite dead.

"Don't!" a voice suddenly pleaded.

Connors.

The FBI agent had managed to get to his feet, still holding his pistol, and stumble toward Santapaola.

"We'll take him into custody!" he said.

"They murdered my son. I cannot wait for federal justice," Santapaola said, spitting on the ground.

Connors raised the pistol, turned it toward the mobster's head.

"I will *have* to shoot you!" he told him.

At that, the men with Santapaola aimed their own weapons at the wounded young FBI agent.

Bartlett and Lyons had now left the dirt shoulder, and were walking toward Connors. Both had their weapons drawn.

"Don't do this, Santapaola!" Bartlett shouted.

"Because of your federal justice system?" Santapaola retorted with great anger. "Is that what you want to tell me?"

"Yes! Give it a chance. Don't sink to the level of the man you want to kill!"

Benedetto Vincenzo Santapaola laughed humorlessly as he pulled the trigger and shot Schmidt through the temple.

"Sicilian justice is quicker!" he said. "Besides, I have been at that level you mention for a very long time already!"

No longer able to stand, Connors fell to his knees, dropping his pistol.

"Get your wounded to the hospital," Santapaola spoke. "That's exactly what *you* should do right now."

Lyons rushed to Connors's side.

Bartlett was sweating, his body drenched despite the nighttime cold.

Finally he lowered his weapon and reholstered it. Santapaola's men, who had kept him in their sights, did the same.

Santapaola strode over to Bartlett.

"You're Stephen Bartlett, aren't you?" he asked.

Bartlett nodded.

"I hear that you are a decent man," Santapaola spoke with apparent admiration. "We could help you regarding *Bloody Winter*, you know."

Benedetto Vincenzo Santapaola knew about the Nazis' secret campaign of destruction!

"But I'm not the one who decides—," Bartlett protested, trying to conceal his astonishment.

"We could help *you*," Santapaola repeated, "but no one else."

"Why me?"

"You once put your own life on the line for some friends of mine . . . partisans in Europe. Now I have to do the same as a point of honor. Or does it surprise you that someone such as myself knows the meaning of the word?"

Bartlett could not speak.

"All you have to do is ask, Stephen Bartlett," Santapaola added, getting some enjoyment out of putting him on the spot. "This is our country, too, and it must *not* be destroyed by those Nazi devils."

He rested one hand on Bartlett's shoulder.

"Take these children back to their homes and leave us now to bury our own," he said with great solemnity, then walked back toward the group waiting for him on the other side of the road.

"We've got them on this," Lyons said excitedly, resting his hand on his pistol. "That bunch has violated federal statues regarding machine guns as well as sawed-off shotguns. And in New Jersey, there happen to be state laws that also preclude the possession of—"

Bartlett faced him.

"Do you realize what 'that bunch' just did?" he interrupted, leaving no room for any doubt about his anger. "The way I look at it, we've witnessed nothing more than self-defense on their part. Remember, they did *not* fire the first shot!"

"But they've got *illegal* firearms!" Lyons persisted. "That makes them fair game in and of itself. Nobody piles up that kind of firepower to go hunting deer, can't you see that? The moment they bought so many weapons, legally or otherwise, they became suspect, opening themselves up for whatever response we bring against them!"

"Put that aside for the moment, Christopher," Bartlett told him, trying to remain calm and think rationally.

"You're talking about letting *criminals* slip through our fingers! How can you even *think* of such a thing?"

"The remaining teenagers from that bus are *alive* as a result! Do you want me to try to arrest the men responsible for saving those kids? I mean, tell me this: What were *we* doing to help?"

"What *could* we do without jeopardizing their lives?"

"I don't argue with that. I don't disagree that Santapaola and his henchmen absolutely represent the worst of the criminal element in this country, and part of the tragedy surrounding them is that they bring unjustified derision upon *all* Italians, fueling the most destructive racist tendencies in this country."

Bartlett was uncomfortably aware of the fact that Hoover himself was not above cracking a racist joke from time to time.

"Right now, though" he went on, "we owe even them *something!* Can't you see that?"

Shaking his head quickly in an exaggerated manner, Lyons spat on the ground in front of Bartlett and walked back toward the car.

The young man who toppled Schmidt and then was knocked nearly unconscious approached Bartlett.

"I overheard, sir," he said. "Thank you for what you said. I wish we could tell those guys over there."

"I don't know if you should play it that way," Bartlett acknowledged. "They *are* murderers and pornographers and much more. They crawl out of their sewers whenever there's anything crooked that they can grab hold of and exploit."

"Sir?" the young man ventured, clearly awkward about doing so.

"Yes?" Bartlett responded.

"I'm a Christian and I believe in forgiveness. That man saved our lives. He deserves our appreciation. Maybe by telling him what's on our hearts, the Lord might use that moment in a special way. You may not feel the same way, but that's how *I* look at it, sir."

Bartlett smiled as he replied, "I, too, am a Christian. You're right. A motive so pure might just do some good. What's your name, son?"

"Jesse Galas. Sir, is it all right with you?"

"I can't stop you, Jesse."

The teenager looked disappointed.

"Nor would I want to," Bartlett added. "Go ahead. See what happens."

Galas smiled and walked over to the other students. They soon returned as a group to where Benedetto Vincenzo Santapaola was getting into an awaiting automobile.

"Sir?" Galas asked with even greater awkwardness.

"What is it?" Santapaola said brusquely.

'Thank you, sir, for saving our lives. I just wanted to let you know that my friends and I will pray for you and your family."

Santapaola's eyes narrowed as he sat there, half in, half out of the black sedan, studying the nervous young man.

"Many I could name curse me," he said. "And now you want to pray for me."

"I can only say how I feel. We're alive because of you. There's no limit to what we owe you, sir."

Galas touched this tough, powerful man gently on the arm.

"That was your son, wasn't it, the little one who was killed earlier?"

Santapaola nodded.

"My much *loved* little boy. Yes, he was."

Santapaola seemed to want to say more but hesitated, which was unusual for him.

"Give me your number, kid," he requested finally. "Maybe we talk again someday."

A bodyguard in the front seat reached through the empty window on that side and handed Galas a pen and a sheet of paper. The teenager nervously scrawled his phone number. As Santapaola was closing the door, Galas added spontaneously, "May God bless you and keep you, sir."

Santapaola's vehicle joined the others in a little procession, most of them except the hearse somehow operational in spite of damage caused by the collisions, though two of them noisily spewed dark smoke from their tailpipes.

For an instant, seventeen-year-old Jesse Galas saw Benedetto Vincenzo Santapaola glance sadly at him, past a few remaining jagged pieces of the rear window. Then, dabbing his blood-shot eyes with a white handkerchief, he slowly turned away.

5

An ambulance arrived within a few minutes and Connors was placed inside.

"It's strange, but, you know, I don't feel too bad," he told Stephen Bartlett and Christopher Lyons just before the rear doors were closed. "I guess it's adrenaline or something. I'm just glad these creeps were stopped before anybody else died."

Lyons shook hands with him and left as another car containing four FBI agents pulled up a short distance away.

"Don't let him get to you," Connors said, his voice abruptly weaker, spittle dribbling out of the corners of his mouth. "He's one of the meanest men I've ever met. Ignore him. Paying any attention to his kind only—"

His face grew pale.

"Can't talk anymore . . . ," he mumbled. "Sir?"

"Yes?" Bartlett asked, bending closer.

"Pray for me, please. There's a lot of pain all of a sudden."

"I'll do just that, Patrick," Bartlett promised.

"Thanks . . ."

Connors started coughing, blood gushing over his chest.

"He's hemorrhaging!" one of the medics yelled. "We've got to get moving, or he's going to die before we make it to the hospital!"

He slammed the door and hurried around to the passenger's side. Bartlett heard him say, "Step on it!"

A rough hand clamped down on his right shoulder.

Christopher Lyons.

"I want Bartlett here placed under arrest," he demanded.

One of the agents, a younger man named James Sommerville, immediately became irritated at Lyons's imperious manner. Dark-haired, blessed with skin that seemed perpetually tanned, with a narrow, well-groomed mustache, dimpled-chin, and a slight scar just above his left eyebrow, he asked, perplexed, "What is the problem?"

"Bartlett decided to let Benedetto Vincenzo Santapaola, of all people, slip right away from us," Lyons told him.

"That *sounds* pretty serious, I admit. But I understand that Hoover himself placed Bartlett in complete charge. That says a lot as far as I am concerned. I can't second-guess the director, that's for sure."

Lyons's eyes flared with rage.

"Yes, but—," he started to say.

"Look, Christopher," interrupted Sommerville, "given that extraordinary departure from normal procedure—someone from another agency allowed such authority—I have to believe that the director obviously has more confidence in Bartlett than you do. Besides, right now, it's Stephen here who's acting like the rational one, not you."

"I'm not going to let him get away with it!" Lyons declared. "I think Bartlett should be thrown into prison."

"Do what you have to, Christopher," replied Sommerville.

Pointedly, he turned his back to Lyons and faced Stephen Bartlett. They could hear the other man muttering as he strode angrily away.

"Anything we can do?" Sommerville asked.

"They were supposed to be heading toward an airfield in this vicinity."

Sommerville, playing with his small mustache for a moment, said, "It seems to me there's an old one less than ten miles from here. It was abandoned years ago. I had forgotten about it until now. But I can't believe the runway is in good enough shape for any plane to land or take off."

"If you forgot about the place, James, then others have too," Bartlett suggested. "And that means it could have become quite a meeting place for Hitler's underground spy system in this country. Do you recall if any hangars were left standing?"

"There were only two small ones to begin with," Sommerville recalled. "The last time I noticed, they were real rusty-looking and gave the impression of being ready to fall over."

"But they could have been repaired from the inside, right?"

"I suppose so."

"While looking as dilapidated as ever from the outside?"

"Of course that could be what happened. But the outward

appearance was so bad that it sure fooled anybody who knew it was there."

"Why wasn't the property snapped up and rebuilt?"

"There was some talk of Farben, that German company—"

Sommerville snapped his fingers as soon as he had said that.

"Farben happens to be one of the leading beneficiaries of slave labor from the concentration camps *and* a top contributor to the National Socialists," Bartlett said. "I bet you're thinking exactly what I am."

"Let's go after them!" Sommerville exclaimed with some enthusiasm. "But do *you* feel able right now? I can imagine how beat you must be after all that's happened."

"Oh, I *am* beat. I would rather hop into bed and sleep for the next twenty-four hours. But I think we may be onto something critical with this. I wonder if there could be more at that airfield than a plane waiting to pick up some saboteurs. It sounds like a perfect spot for them to conduct their business in absolute secrecy."

"Surrounded by miles of pine barrens!"

Over the years, remnants of settlements from colonial times had been found at Batsto, New Jersey, and other places, with evidence of Indian dwellings dating back ever longer.

"I wish we had more agents," Bartlett said regretfully. "We don't know what we're going to run into."

"If we wait for reinforcements, then by the time we get them here," Sommerville suggested, "that plane may be long gone. I don't think they'll keep on waiting indefinitely. At some point they're going to realize that something isn't right, and take off."

Several patrol cars with New Jersey State Police officers had arrived on the scene. One of them, a sergeant, walked over to Bartlett and Sommerville.

"Aren't you Stephen Bartlett?" he asked.

"I am. What am I guilty of this time?"

The trooper chuckled as he said, "I don't know if that's the way I'd put it, sir."

"Spit it out, sergeant."

"Sir, I heard about what you did to rescue your family from Dachau."

"I made the only choice I could have," Bartlett told him. "I don't think you would have acted differently to protect your own loved ones."

"You're probably right. But it was more than that, I think, sir. You went right into the lion's den, and you tried to help others at the same time. A couple of our fly-boys are alive because of what you did."

Feeling self-conscious, he cleared his throat before adding, "What I'm trying to say, and I'm not doing it all that well, is that I admire you for your courage, sir."

He looked from Bartlett to Sommerville.

"Anything we can do to help?" the policeman asked. "I have half a dozen very well armed officers here. And I can summon twice that many in a few minutes if necessary."

Bartlett's answer was immediate.

The pine barrens in those days were among the most deserted areas east of the Mississippi and the most isolated, encompassing an astonishing percentage of New Jersey. Roads slicing through the barrens were often not in the best condition.

During Prohibition, moonshiners would set up their stills in this area and turn out nearly as much liquor as the distilleries had done before they were shut down. Few were apprehended, largely because mafioso influence in New Jersey had always reached up to even the governor's office. But an additional factor was that the inaccessibility of anybody who wanted to do *anything* secretly in the midst of the barrens was pretty much guaranteed.

During this time and later, tiny New Jersey also found itself the dumping ground for victims of the gangland wars of the twenties and into the thirties.

Location: the pine barrens.

"It seems so obvious that the Nazis would attempt a base of operations here," Bartlett whispered as he crouched down less than half a mile west of the airfield, his position hidden but still allowing a good view of the spot. "And yet nobody from any agency or department has ever thought to comb this area."

That was one of several implausibilities that were beginning to bother him.

"How *easily* spies are *still* getting into this country!" he exclaimed. "I mean, we're at war, and yet the stream seems to be continuing. How do they do it? What sort of genius was Wilhelm Canaris?"

Sommerville paused thoughtfully, then nodded in agreement as he said, "Of course, after the sweep of the late thirties and early forties, everyone at the agency, including, eh, the director himself, assumed there would be no more concentrated activity from any underground spy network. It was then thought to have been rendered ineffectual, or at least that was the conventional wisdom a couple of years ago."

Bartlett glanced at his new comrade.

"Is there something else, James?" he asked.

"I worry about some things," Sommerville acknowledged, keeping his voice low.

"What things?"

"Within the bureau itself."

Bartlett's palms were suddenly sweaty.

"Bad agents?" he asked. "Is that what you mean?"

"Yes . . ."

"Working both sides of the street?"

"I mean, tell me this: What other explanation could there be for the kinds of unfathomable misjudgments we've just been talking about? And the continuing influx of spies, as you said. We've only scratched the surface, as it turns out. If we win the war, what will happen to those who've never been caught? Will they be like a dormant cancer, ready to spread throughout the land when another master commands them to do so?

"After all, Hoover isn't a stupid man, and he's thoroughly honest, whatever else you could say about him. But he, like the rest of us, can act only on the basis of the information that is provided to him."

"Are you suggesting that sometimes he doesn't get all the facts?" Bartlett asked with a touch of sarcasm.

"It seems that way on occasion," confessed Sommerville. Look at what happened during World War I."

"Black Tom? Is that what you mean?"

"You got that right!" Sommerville said. "Anybody with any insight, any brains, would realize that if Germany's spies were capable of blowing up an important munitions depot just outside New York City, along with twenty-eight incidents at other places in just that general area alone, just what is going to be possible thirty-odd years later, with all that those guys have surely learned about explosives and such in the meantime?"

"There's another possibility, you know," Bartlett offered.

"What could it be?"

"That Hoover's enemies in Congress are intent upon sabotaging him."

"But in doing that, they could end up doing in the country as a whole!" Sommerville exclaimed.

Bartlett chuckled cynically.

"Yet should what some people are capable of be so surprising anymore?" he hinted. "Look at the suspicions about Roosevelt."

"You mean the possibility that he got us into war with the Japanese as a last-ditch effort to end the depression and therefore boost his political fortunes?"

"Exactly what I mean! He's been entrenched so long, with a government packed full of his cronies, that it's understandable he doesn't want to let go and give the Republicans a shot at the White House."

"Wickedness in high places . . . ," Sommerville mused softly.

"Could be a real good example of that, I'm afraid."

Two agents who had gone ahead to reconnoiter the area were now returning, their faces flushed.

"You would not believe what that gang has going for them up ahead!" one of them exclaimed.

An airfield, yes, and a plane that had been readied for immediate takeoff. But that was only part of what the agents had found.

"I hate to say it," one of them remarked, "but they've been thumbing their noses at our internal security measures for a long time. They didn't accumulate all the stuff we saw in just a few weeks!"

Stored at the airfield had been a considerable storehouse of weapons—rifles, machine guns, pistols, grenades, bazookas—as well as ammunition.

"We could spot only part of their cache," he said. "There's probably more, and I suspect they've hidden the rest underground."

Along with the weapons, they saw several very large canisters of silver paint.

"Isn't that crazy?" the other FBI agent said. "What's so special about paint of any color? We saw some of those guys pouring it from one of the canisters into what looked like ordinary cans. What are we to make of that? It seems so pointless."

"So we worry only about the kinds of weapons they have, nothing else!" exclaimed Sommerville.

"We go in now," Bartlett said. "Is everyone with me on this?"

The agents and the state police officers raised their hands in agreement.

"Let's head out," Bartlett told him.

The plan Bartlett had offered was nearly identical to the one he had put into action months ago between Jewish partisans and himself before they began to attack the Dachau concentration camp: A group of policemen would be stationed at each of the four corners of the airfield, taking an FBI agent along with them. If they were met with gunfire, they would respond in kind.

"We just happen to have a small box filled with some sticks of dynamite," one of the policemen had told Bartlett. "It's in the trunk of one of the cars."

"Pure coincidence, I guess," another added. "The guys we nabbed had it to protect their booze stills. We didn't have time to dispose of the stuff before we got a call about the school bus. And now look at what we're doing!"

6

More than a dozen men could be seen moving various cartons and other containers, some with wire straps and reinforced wooden edges, from the two hangars onto the awaiting trucks. The pace of their activity showed that they were aware there was very little time left to abandon that location before the Feds descended upon it.

Several were quite young, perhaps in their late teens. When an adult approached one of them, he would click his heels together salute by stretching out his right arm and saying something, undoubtedly "Heil Hitler!"

Their faces! Bartlett exclaimed to himself. *They seem almost like men possessed. Each one has the look of a Himmler or a Goebbels or the* Führer *himself! And the teenagers seem the same: all evidence of their youth is gone.*

A hardness to their features.

He shuddered to think of these boys, shorn of the idealism typical of their age, finding themselves in any situation that required some sense of mercy.

They would be no different than the guards at the camps, he decided, *cold, unyielding, and barbaric in their cruelty.*

Apparently James Sommerville felt the same. He tapped Bartlett on the shoulder and imitated the teenagers' well-nigh glazed look.

Some of the cartons obviously contained weapons. But others were filled with parts that could be assembled to make equipment that seemed to range from shortwave radios to makeshift but brutally effective bombs.

Where are they heading? he wondered. *We need to know!*

He leaned over and whispered to Sommerville, "I think we should let one truck supposedly get away from us, but before we do we'll have to rig it with a tracer box. We can't follow close behind it or they'll get suspicious before very long."

He turned and looked around at the other men.

"Anybody here have something like a tracer box?" he asked, though not very hopefully. "These guys are obviously intending to start something big here. I'd love to find out what their destination is."

"Evans?" Sommerville, smiling slightly, spoke as he motioned with his right hand.

"Be right back, sir . . . ," someone answered him, then quickly left the group, returning several minutes later with a two-inch-by-three-inch black metal box, a flat, thin gray magnet protruding from one side of it.

"Does Hoover think of everything?" Bartlett asked.

"It's one of his charming traits," the agent remarked, deadpan.

"Consider me a volunteer," Sommerville spoke up. "With any luck, I can dash on in there, plant it under one of the trucks, and get back here without anyone seeing me. When that truck pulls out, I can be waiting to follow it at some distance."

"And I'll make sure Hoover has a crack team ready to dispatch once you find out where they've stopped."

"Sounds like a good plan," the other man agreed.

The group of agents and troopers advanced slowly, finally coming within two or three hundred feet of the barbed-wire fence, shielding themselves from view behind trees or bushes and other undergrowth.

Ahead of them, the airfield was surrounded by another barbed-wire fence, this one six feet high. Beyond it were the two small hangars and the plane, plus four flatbed trucks and two rusty, old sedans.

A large, heavy container slipped as it was being carried from the hangar—grenades and smaller boxes of shells spilling onto the runway.

"Something's going to be happening any day now," Sommerville remarked, hugging himself for a moment. "Don't you get that feeling?"

"Unless they're just relocating everything they have, knowing that the guys on the school bus are supposed to be headed here," Bartlett said, "and are certain to be followed."

Bartlett knew that he had to be careful not to reveal anything he had learned about the so-called *Bloody Winter* operation even to an FBI agent. Only J. Edgar Hoover and William Casey could be considered "safe" listeners.

"I hear the Nazis have been planning for a major operation that's supposed to happen some time soon," he whispered vaguely.

"You're thinking this could be part of it?" Sommerville remarked.

"I do, and I begin to wonder how many other isolated places like this one are being appropriated all across the country."

He could envision locations ideal for their purposes in the forest areas of Oregon and Washington State or the mountainous regions of Missouri.

"All in preparation for—," Sommerville said.

"Look at how the boxes are being designated," Bartlett interrupted.

One had been marked *Denver.* On another was written *New Orleans.*

Of course! Bartlett exclaimed silently. *There are various spots across the Louisiana swamps and bayous that no one other than Cajuns has seen until now.*

Dozens of cartons destined for as many places.

"Look!" Sommerville whispered as he pointed.

Three men were starting to board the plane. After they were inside, the propellers started turning, but it didn't take off.

"They're having trouble, I think," remarked Sommerville.

One of them jumped out and started to argue rather violently with another man who had hurried over to examine the engine.

"Wait a moment!" Bartlett exclaimed, nearly failing to keep his voice low. "I recognize one of those guys."

"Who is it?" Sommerville asked.

"If I'm right, he's Benton Grantham, a top aide to one of the senators who had been campaigning most loudly and persistently for nonintervention, calling it Europe's war, not ours. He's had to change what is intended for public consumption as a result of Pearl Harbor and the grotesque revelations coming out of the European theater, but I wonder how much of that is only surface stuff. In any event, the scuttlebutt is that Grantham's interest in the senator happened to be more than political."

"If Grantham's on Berlin's payroll, then I wonder what might be going on as far as the senator himself is concerned?"

As he spoke, Sommerville looked as though he was becoming ill.

"If what we're saying is more than just speculation," he continued, "if there is any truth at all in it, then that means the enemy's gotten so deep into the muscle and the bone of this country, well, I wonder if we'll ever find out about who the rest of them are before they've done America a whole lot of harm!"

"We shouldn't be surprised," Bartlett mused. "After all, look at what a Nazi-loving creep Lindbergh turned out to be."

One of the trucks was already heading toward a gate at the south end of the barbed-wire enclosure.

"Get another before it's too late," Bartlett told him.

"I'm out of here!" Sommerville muttered.

"Later, take someone with you when you start tracking it."

"No time for that, sir! You'll need everybody else here. Don't worry. I'll play it safe. I definitely don't want my wife to become a widow anytime soon. She's pregnant . . . our first child . . . due to enter this world any day now. I can't wait to hold the little guy in my arms. *That's* where everything comes together if you ask me!"

"As God intended," Bartlett agreed.

The two men shook hands, then Sommerville darted up to the fence, used some clippers to snap apart three strands of barbed wire, and slipped through.

The truck nearest him was to his left a hundred feet or so.

As he was about to run up to it, a tall man with very broad shoulders and a sizable reddish beard, came around the other side.

For a split second the two looked at one another, then the bearded one started to reach for a pistol under his sheepskin jacket.

Sommerville sprang at him and sent his considerable bulk sprawling with a karate kick to the midsection, but stumbled and fell back against the truck. The bearded man jumped to his feet with surprising speed and lunged for the FBI agent.

Bartlett and the others had already attached silencers to the barrels of their Colts. He stretched out both arms, each helping to steady the other, aimed at the big man, and pulled the trigger, catching him in the back, between his shoulder blades, the impact smashing him face-forward against the truck. He turned painfully, his nose broken, blood spilling from his nostrils, and then fell forward, bouncing slightly as he hit the ground.

Sommerville dashed back to the truck, stuck the tracer unit just behind the rear bumper, and started to run toward the fence.

"Klaus is hit!" a man shouted as he came out from the hangar, his hands loaded with grenades.

He dropped all but one, pulled the plug, and tossed it at Sommerville. It exploded some distance away, but the blast still knocked the FBI agent off his feet.

Slightly dazed but otherwise unaffected, Sommerville stood and made it the rest of the way to the fence, signaling to the others that he was okay. Then he turned left and headed toward where they had parked their cars.

As the man was reaching down for another grenade, he was hit by three shots, two in his stomach and another in his temple.

Grantham, the senator's aide, still standing outside the plane, suddenly seemed terrified and confused and made a dash for the door on the other side but found it locked.

"You *cannot* leave without me!" he screamed, veins bulging on his forehead.

The propellers started to spin, then sputtered.

Bartlett got to his feet, lighting a stick of dynamite.

For an instant, Grantham saw him, a look of hatred freezing his face.

As Bartlett threw the dynamite, the aide turned and ran toward the truck under which Sommerville had placed the tracking device. The reddish, nine-inch, round stick landed under the plane's tail section. For a moment, there was a lull, then the plane was shattered into hundreds of pieces, anything other than metal now ablaze, some of the fragments shooting straight up into the air. As these pieces plummeted back, a number of saboteurs were hit, setting their clothes on fire. Two other men were frantically trying to put out flames that had started in their hair.

Those drums of paint also proved highly combustible, one after the other exploding as bullets punctured them, sending out gushers of fire like lava from a volcano.

Having already cut open a larger section of the fence, Bartlett led the FBI agents and state police onto the airfield.

A previously unseen sniper crouching on the roof of one of the two plane hangars caught a state policeman in the shoulder but was spotted immediately and brought down by a barrage of shots from four of the policemen.

One by one, the vehicles were blown up. Only that single truck had been allowed to stand intact.

Grantham and three other men were now inside, trying to get it started. A policeman was about to fire at them, but Bartlett grabbed his arm and stopped him.

"I *want* them to *escape!*" he snapped. "Agent Sommerville's going to track where they'll be heading."

The police officer apologized.

"I just got caught up in this," he said. "Sorry, sir. I knew it as well as you did."

Finally the motor started, and the truck began speeding toward the airfield's single open gate, dodging spot fires and debris from the devastated trucks and large drums of paint, some of which were spilling their contents onto the asphalt.

Abruptly it swerved into one of the fence posts, then whoever was driving seemed to regain control and it continued on, past the gate, and onto the dirt road that was the airfield's only link to the main highway in that area.

Seven of the saboteurs surrendered; except for the men in the truck the rest had been killed during the attack.

Bartlett walked down the line they formed, pausing briefly in front of each one.

He came to one of the boys, a handsome sixteen-year-old with red hair, some freckles, and cold, dead eyes like the others.

"What's your name?" he asked.

"Matthew," came the reluctant reply, spoken in a tone as lifeless as his eyes.

"You've thrown away your life because of hatred fed to you by others," Bartlett said with great pity. "Yet you have a mind that gives you the ability to reason things out. How could this have happened, son? How could you have fallen for the delusion of a sick group of men running the war from their fortress in Berlin?

"Don't *ever* call me 'son,'" Matthew growled. "You defend the rights of Jews. That makes you scum under my feet."

"Have you ever *seen* an extermination camp?" Bartlett asked.

"I haven't. But I look forward to it someday."

"Did you know that Heinrich Himmler threw up after spending an afternoon at one of them? The architect of the "Final Solution" couldn't stand seeing the fruits of his own policy. He has been having nightmares ever since."

"Lies!" the teenager screamed. "He is *proud* of what he has accomplished. Besides, how would *you* know? I'm not so stupid to fall for your tricks."

He grabbed the boy by the neck.

"Because I was in Dachau. Your Nazi heroes took my wife and son and were about to let Mengele experiment on them. But I got there in time, and with God's help—"

"God would *never* be on your side! He would want *us* to succeed by cleansing the world of those filthy betrayers of His Son. I hate the *Juden* swine because I love Jesus."

Bartlett let go, looking at the teenager sadly.

"What about the countless Jewish children, even babies, who are thrown in the crematoriums? Sometimes they're not quite dead while this is happening. I've held what was left of their tiny bones in my hands, hands covered with the white dust of many more.

"What about Mengele, who tried to graft two Gypsy babies together in a mindless experiment to *create* Siamese twins? He opened up their abdomens, took out the kidneys of one child, sewed their intestines together, and shoved them into a *cage* while he stood by and waited to see how long it would take them to die. He never really thought either of them had any chance to live. It was simply a bit of idle scientific curiosity on his part! That's what he told someone, you know, *idle curiosity!*"

Matthew winced at that, looking away from Bartlett.

"You say that you love Jesus," he continued. "But what about that afternoon when Jesus had children all around Him, balancing them on His knees, running His fingers through their soft young hair? Those were *Jewish* babies, Matthew. He said that it would be better for anyone bringing harm to even a single one of them to not have been born or that a millstone be tied around that person's neck and he be thrown in the deepest sea."

Matthew was looking at him again.

"Remember this, if you will allow yourself: Vast numbers of Jewish children have perished in the camps," Bartlett told him "They were either gassed or shot in the back of the head or allowed to starve to death or given over to the degenerate sexual habits of guards like Ivan the Terrible and others or killed by diseases that have been spreading throughout Auschwitz, Mauthausen, Treblinka, and others.

"Such men have done far, far more than merely *harm* those helpless little ones Jesus talked about with so much tenderness. And you know what? They have not stopped at a single child or a dozen or a hundred. If you love Jesus, you must *hate* these monsters; you must *hate* the fact that you are being poured into the same stinking mold that formed them."

His nose was less than a inch away from the teenager's.

"I want to know *now*, Matthew: How *can* you claim to love the

Son of God and want to be like the men who have the blood of Jewish children on their hands?"

The teenager used his finger in an obscene gesture and then spat at Bartlett.

Bartlett had to restrain himself, had to fight the welling desire to beat this young Nazi nearly to death as though that somehow would wrench out of the boy the corruption that had seized hold of his very soul.

But he did nothing of the sort. He just turned and headed toward the hangars, anger and loathing making him sweat even during that cool October morning. He heard Matthew call after him, "I will still be accepted by Jesus at the gates of heaven, whether you like it or not. He'll smile at me and say, 'Well done, good and faithful servant. All of heaven bids you welcome. Your rewards are waiting.'"

Bartlett kept walking, pretending not to be affected, pretending to ignore those compelling, haunting words.

. . . *I will still be accepted by Jesus at the gates of heaven.*

He reached the hangar and leaned against the corrugated metal side to steady himself. Behind him, a voice that he recognized as Matthew's was shouting obscenities before it finally was cut off, and only the crackling sounds of the remaining flames reached his ears.

7

4:15 A.M.

It was obvious, as Stephen Bartlett surveyed that one hangar, that the saboteurs had only begun the task of clearing out its contents. Whatever warning they had gotten by whatever means had not come quickly enough, and they ran out of time.

Numerous boxes of varying size and durability remained, along with dark wooden file cabinets and sacks resembling shopping bags with thin jute handles. All were packed with staplers, rubber bands, paper clips, hand stamps, erasers, and other office items.

They were more concerned with their arsenal, he told himself. *Everything else understandably tended to take second place.*

Nor had they progressed very far with the transferring of that arsenal. Either more trucks were supposed to be sent to the airfield, or the new location was close enough to allow round trips in a fairly short time.

He poked around idly, wondering what might be turned up that he could take back to Hoover and Casey.

His foot kicked against something.

A shoebox.

Inside were little pamphlets.

He picked up one and flipped through the pages, some bile from his stomach coming up in his mouth, burning his throat, as he read the text.

"'How to skin a Jew' . . . ," he read out loud. "'The ones with rather elaborate tattoos provide the most attractive lampshades. It is preferable that they are dead when the operation starts. Granted that hearing their cries of agony can be very enjoyable, and, for that reason, there is always the temptation to keep them alive while it is

65

being done, but the skin is in better shape if it is saturated with less blood and not subjected to the stress that a reluctant subject would impose upon it. This only results in an inferior product. Of course, the Jew in each case could be sedated but that wouldn't solve the blood problem, and he might die anyway."

. . . *which only results in an inferior product.*

Tears of rage stung his eyes and he had to squint as he looked for the name of the author. He wasn't surprised when he found it.

Ilse Koch . . . nicknamed the Bitch of Buchenwald by those who knew and loathed the infamous woman.

Bartlett would have crumpled up that little pamphlet and disposed of it in one of the fires outside but it was the only copy as far as he could tell, and he needed to pile up as much evidence as he could find.

To dump on the hand-carved mahogany desk of Benton Grantham's boss!

He had to admit that that wild, extravagant thought held some appeal for him and, undoubtedly, it would for Hoover as well. So he put it back in the box, noticing the other degrading topics named on the covers of additional pamphlets.

A policeman stepped inside the hangar to ask if he needed any help.

"Got a box here," he said. "Why don't you make sure it's kept safe for me?"

"Interesting stuff there?"

"I don't know if 'interesting' is the right word. Disgusting is better!"

The policeman walked over to him, and reached out for the box.

"Top secret, sir, or can I glance through it?" he asked.

"You can look, but you may regret it."

"Nothing fazes me these days, sir."

He seemed to want to say something else.

Bartlett waited, signaling that he would be glad to listen.

"May I speak freely, sir?" the officer asked, showing by his manner that he was still uncertain.

"Go right ahead," Bartlett, smiling, reassuring him.

"In my job I see unimaginable filth, and then I go to church every Sunday and hear about the depravity of the human soul. Not too long ago, I worshiped where the pastor talked on and on about man's innate goodness.

"Can you believe that? You were in the midst of a kind of hell yourself when you served in Europe. To think that, given the stories we're hearing about those extermination camps, a minister of the gospel chooses to cling to such idle fantasies! I mean, I hear he hasn't changed his tune a bit even now.

"If I were still a member of that congregation, I would challenge the guy to do what I do and see what I see and still try somehow to convince himself that human nature is so naturally fine and good and all the rest. Every day what I witness contradicts that stupid notion."

He took the shoebox, nodded somewhat sheepishly, and told Bartlett not to hesitate to ask for assistance if needed.

"Whatever's in here, I can handle," he added with more confidence.

Then he started to leaf through the assorted contents as he slowly walked out of the hangar.

Seconds later, Bartlett heard the man groan, then saw him rush behind a large pile of debris.

Approaching sunrise . . .

The truck carrying senatorial aide Benton Grantham and the other men headed toward the shore south of Ocean City, New Jersey, passing through the farming community of Vineland, and then, Millville, Egg Harbor, Mays Landing, and other colonial-era towns, ultimately ending up at an isolated spot a few miles near Wildwood.

The driver has enough sense to realize that any speeding would bring attention to them, James Sommerville thought. *So he's driving legally—and probably sweating out every mile!*

The truck was driven onto the beach, stopping less than fifty feet from the water's edge.

The four men jumped out and hurried to the back of the truck where they unloaded some boxes.

Then they sat down on the sand and waited.

Sommerville had parked down the road, which was lined by hut-shaped beach houses on his left and the shore on his right. Obviously this was an extension of a community that came to life only during the summer months and seemed in forlorn hibernation any other time of year, becoming cold and bleak in late October, when sudden, chill winds kicked up and howled like mournful banshees.

He carried a Tommy gun and extra ammo in addition to his regular-caliber pistol, the latter in a holster strapped to his side. He knew he could handle the four of them since they seemed to have taken little firepower with them, from the airfield—though there was no way of knowing what had been loaded earlier onto the truck.

He radioed in his location and made sure that those other FBI agents he had been promised would be dispatched immediately to help him.

What are they waiting for? Sommerville asked himself as he crouched in a ditch beside the road and looked at them through some straggly plants that nevertheless hid him from view. *They've just stopped.*

Occasionally, the men would break their own silence and talk in low voices, chuckling a bit for some reason unknown to Sommerville.

"What a pity we had to leave so much behind," Grantham was saying.

"Don't be concerned with the munitions," another man told him. "They can be easily replaced. The Allies may not realize it yet, but German factories aided by Jew labor are turning out more bombs, grenades, and guns now than when the war started.

"The rest of the stuff was mostly training manuals and pamphlets aimed at the American masses, for the Nazis know they hate Negros and Jews and others they blame for corrupting the Puritan spirit that once formed the backbone of this nation."

Grantham snorted as he glanced at his watch.

"They should be here soon," he commented nervously.

"I hope so," the other man said. "If the Feds find out—"

"Hey, nobody followed us. They were too busy with the others. We have nothing to worry about now."

"Look!"

They all turned toward the ocean.

Something caught their attention, something dark and brutish in its appearance, massive and threatening.

A gray-black shape rising from the water.

Sommerville saw it also and had to restrain himself from reacting audibly.

Very large, this hulking presence in the early-morning light seemed like some grotesque and brutish predator breaking the foam-laced surf.

The four men on the beach waited anxiously until it had completely surfaced.

A German U-boat!

Sommerville's mind was reeling.

He knew of other U-boat sightings but none had been reported to be so close, and never in the vicinity of the New Jersey shoreline.

Three men came up on the deck of the ship, responding in like manner as the four on shore clicked their heels together, their right arms shooting up, their voices clear and loud, calling out, "*Heil Hitler!*"

A small inflatable raft was shoved over the side by another crew member.

In just over a minute, the Germans were on the beach, warmly greeting Benton Grantham and his three companions.

I've got to get through to Bartlett or somebody else, Sommerville thought. This is far bigger than any of us imagined. That sub has enough firepower to blow away—

He grabbed the Tommy and hurried back to the car. Once inside, he radioed an urgent message, hoping Stephen Bartlett hadn't yet left the airfield.

Still there.

"Hello, James," Bartlett's voice came over the unit. "Did you track them—?"

"Sorry, sir, but I've got to make this fast!" Sommerville interrupted.

He told Bartlett what was happening.

"I think they are transferring massive amounts of documents. Someone has alerted them to what was going to happen at the airfield. If the airfield represented a major nerve center for their clandestine operations in the United States, then they must have had an incredible wealth of papers there: names, addresses, phone numbers, maps—you can only imagine what else!"

"Yes. They left behind the relatively unimportant stuff," Bartlett told him. "Some of it's pretty grisly but not strategic."

"And now they're loading it onto the sub," Sommerville continued, "which will then take it either back to Berlin or drop it off at some other point along the Eastern seaboard. But why is Grantham present?"

"That only emphasizes the importance of this location. He must have come to supervise everything, to make sure the most crucial stuff is not left behind."

"A Nazi spy highly placed in the U.S. Senate!" Sommerville remarked. "How many more of them are there?"

"Please, James, stay out of their way!" Bartlett pleaded. "Each of us is susceptible to the temptation to be a hero or a coward in such a situation. Be neither. Observe but don't interfere until we get there. Is that understood?"

Sommerville assured him it was.

"I'm going to see how we can move some heavy-duty equipment quickly out to where you are, either through the Coast Guard or the Navy. We can't let that sub slip away. And James . . . ?"

"Yes sir?"

"I'm going to pull everyone out of the airfield here, and we'll be getting to you as fast as we can. Remember, don't take any unnecessary risks!"

"Agreed," Sommerville told him. "May God speed you, sir."

The connection was broken.

Sommerville sat for several seconds, still holding the microphone in his hand, sweet little memories of his wife suddenly stirring his mind as he considered what the next few hours would bring.

Bartlett spoke little after bringing the agents and state police together and telling them what had developed.

"If they can't retreat by sea," one of the agents remarked, "they may try to escape by land. That would only mean more hostages, more bloodshed. They'd have no qualms about torching entire neighborhoods."

"I've already called William Casey, my boss, as well as Director Hoover," Bartlett told him, "and both have pledged any amount of support necessary. In fact, Casey told me, 'Whatever it takes to get this done!'"

He turned to the state police.

"From now on, it's clearly the responsibility of the federal government. None of you has any obligation to go along."

An older officer with bushy gray eyebrows stepped forward.

"Sir, what you say is true," he acknowledged, "but no one knows how long it will take for a contingent of forces to get here. In wartime, all efforts are focused on the battlefield. Everything back home is geared toward *there*. It's uncertain at this point how fast a strained military establishment could act."

Bartlett was impressed by this man.

"What's your name?" he asked.

"Clancy, sir, Clancy Bergen. Right now, we're maybe an hour away from Sommerville's location, not that much if we break all the speed limits. The less time lost, the more the chance we can draw a net around those traitors. I think I can say, for everyone here, that our country means a lot more to us than jurisdictional protocol."

"And we need to make sure nothing happens to Sommerville!" an FBI agent shouted. "We can't leave him in the hands of the bureaucracy."

Bartlett agreed, a decision he had already made himself but knew would work better if everyone participated with unanimity.

"Let's go!' he exclaimed, glad that the time for talking had passed.

8

After sunrise . . .

Fifty-eight-year-old, potbellied Casey Aldrich had been serving as a volunteer pilot with the Civil Air Patrol since its formation in 1941 as part of the Office of Civilian Defense. The agency had come about because the nation's regular military forces were almost entirely stationed in the European and Asian theaters of operation and some additional security manpower was needed within the United States itself.

Aldrich continued with CAP after it was transferred to the War Department in 1943, when it became an auxiliary of the Army Air Corps and routinely participated in air patrols along the Eastern seaboard from the northern end of the Jersey shore on down to Cape Hatteras, North Carolina.

He enjoyed flying at sunrise, when striking colors lapped over his two-seat Cessna as he tried to keep his attention on the offshore area below. During such moments, he felt more at peace than at any other time in his life. Sometimes he flew with a copilot next to him; other times he was alone but not at all lonesome, his mind clear, his emotions cleansed.

Aldrich was alone that late-October morning, his regular copilot, a neighborhood friend, having suffered a broken arm a week earlier.

You're not missing anything, Jake! he thought. *Routine stuff . . . I bet the Nazis have finally given up and pulled back their subs permanently.*

Aldrich felt periodic feelings of inferiority that he wasn't at the battlefront with the American troops, a fact that had nothing to do with his masculinity or his courage, yet everything to do with his age.

Still, he had to deal with emotions that battered him every time he read about someone he knew dying in France or Italy or Germany or elsewhere, on the ground during battle or as an aircraft was knocked out of the sky.

So many of my friends have been shot, blown to bits by grenades, run over by tanks, he recalled. *They've been captured, tortured, beaten to death. And yet here I am, safe, secure, with plenty to eat and a familiar bed to sleep in and my wife's warm body beside me.*

CAP succeeded in giving back to Casey Aldrich some of his personal sense of respectability, made him feel as though he were contributing in some way, however marginally. Then, as U-boat sightings had started to increase a year or so earlier, he had felt that his worth to his country went up in direct proportion.

And yet sometimes, on quiet mornings, with nothing but the familiar, deserted shoreline below, boredom grabbed him. Aldrich felt useless again, doing conscience-salving make-work that added up to nothing real or substantial, especially with the U-boat sightings apparently going back down again.

Lord, he prayed, *I don't want my wife and two boys to lose their respect for me. The kids see that the fathers of their buddies are fighting in Europe, but their old man is still at home tending to the family grocery business and, oh yeah, he spends a few hours a week in some old plane with a few grenades and a couple of rifles as weapons.*

He sighed as he radioed back to headquarters that everything was okay, then started to turn the Cessna around and head back.

Something caught the early-morning sun, reflecting it strongly enough to make him avert his eyes.

An instant later, Aldrich glanced back at the same spot.

As his vision cleared, he could see directly ahead a number of scurrying figures on a strand of beach, a truck . . . and in somewhat shallow water not far from shore . . . *a U-boat!*

Aldrich felt his stomach tighten.

None of the others had come so close to shore. Now this one did just that, and the enemy had actually disembarked and set foot on land.

"This is my country!" Aldrich yelled out loud. "You can't do this. You can't—"

His impulse was to act drastically as he noticed boxes being loaded onto it the sub and others being taken off and placed on shore, a dozen men scurrying about, all but four of them in the uniforms of the German Navy.

They may be gone by the time reinforcements come, he told himself. *They do whatever it is that they're up to and then sneak away!*

His palms became sweaty as he reached for the microphone.

"Need help!" he murmured into it, then went on to describe what he had spotted.

"Fly past them, Casey," the order came. "Do nothing until we can get more planes out there, and whatever else we can throw at them."

"Roger and out," Aldrich said, then broke the connection.

He increased his altitude drastically so that as he flew over them, they would be more likely to assume he had gone by without noticing the sub's presence or the workmen's activity.

What if there is a delay . . . if those Germans reboard the sub and it starts to pull away from shore before—?

He saw jetties at the northern and southern ends of the beach, giving it a covelike setting.

They'd have to head straight out, he reasoned. *In this location two routes of escape are cut off to them. But they must have figured that they would never be sighted.*

He banged his fist against the dashboard over the instrument panel.

"The *arrogance!*" he snarled out loud. "You won't get away with it this time. That's a promise. You won't!"

Aldrich recalled those merchant marine vessels and others that had been sunk or damaged as a result of being confronted by U-boats off the East Coast of the United States. He thought of the desperation that had led to the illustrious *Queen Elizabeth II*'s being converted from a cruise ship to an elaborately camouflaged troop-and-supply vessel. With the hope that the Nazis wouldn't see through her cover, the ship's military crew now made each journey wondering if the truth had become known and another tragedy would play itself out on the Atlantic Ocean.

Aldrich knew that a number of CAP volunteers happened to live in the area. Not all had duties as pilots. But they served anyway as mechanics or by manning shortwave units or doing whatever else was needed.

Most were farmers. A couple were ministers. One was a retired army colonel. Another had been a munitions expert during World War I. Others were accountants, doctors, attorneys, mail carriers, businessmen.

If the commander and his crew are blocked off from a retreat by sea, they may hit land . . . if they don't surrender . . .

His mind suddenly filled with images of individual farmhouses in flames, the main streets of small rural communities littered with overturned cars, glass, and chunks of metal . . . and along with this, men, women and children slaughtered or taken hostage.

What of the Jews? he wondered. *This area is loaded with retired Jewish couples. Some have started little farms. Others—*

Aldrich could envision ghastly encounters with the intruders from that U-boat, most often defenseless old men and women subjected to brief but fatal and grisly outbursts of the insatiable Nazi thirst for the spilling of "impure" Jewish blood that had drenched Europe, now transplanted to tiny New Jersey.

Oh, Lord, Lord, he prayed, *don't let it be like that here! Use me as You see fit to help avoid the horrors. I'll do whatever You ask, go wherever You lead.*

He hesitated, tears coming without shame, then added, *But please, Lord, see to my loved ones if anything happens to me. Take care of my wife, my sons!*

Suddenly very much aware of what had to be done, Casey Aldrich closed his eyes for a moment, his head pounding as he reached for the shortwave unit's microphone and made the first call.

"Arnie . . . ," he said a few seconds later, his voice more calm than he thought would have been possible. "There's something you gotta do, and you gotta do it right away."

James Sommerville knew he could not wait any longer.

Activity on the beach was beginning to wind down. Only a few more containers were left to be loaded onto the U-boat.

The German captain was talking animatedly in English with Benton Grantham.

"They will be fooled," he gloated. "When they think they have it all figured out, we will slip the Americans a very big surprise."

"I think I have been seen, you know," Grantham told him impatiently. "I will have to go into hiding."

"We can arrange that. Don't worry. You will be contacted in a day or two."

"The usual place?"

The captain nodded.

"We must leave in a few minutes," he said. "The tide will be going out soon. If we don't make it now, we'll be stuck here."

That was when the old Cessna came into view again.

Sommerville had seen it a short while before and had dismissed it as unimportant, never expecting the pilot to be aware enough of what was happening to want to pay a return visit.

What is he doing? wondered the FBI agent. *He can't be thinking he's any match for a German submarine!*

Those on the beach also were gazing up at the plane.

"It is a mindless gnat, and we are the elephant," the captain sneered.

"I don't think so." A sweating Grantham dared to contradict him. "You see, the Civil Air Patrol has been around here and—"

"You suggest that it might be one of *them?*" the captain interrupted as he broke out into coarse laughter. "We've seen their kind before. The pilots are rejects. They couldn't make it into the regular armed forces."

He waved over one of the crew members.

"Blast him out of the sky!" he ordered.

The other man saluted, then ran up to the water's edge, signaling to someone stationed on the deck of the U-boat. The sailor then scrambled down into the vessel, returning with a light artillery weapon they had brought along for just such a purpose since they knew they had to be prepared for being discovered, despite their best covert preparations.

Sommerville could not recognize what model it was from such a distance, noting simply that it seemed bulky and powerful-looking, certainly adequate against a much more combat-worthy plane than the Cessna. If hit by a projectile from it, the little two-seater Cessna undoubtedly would be shattered into countless numbers of pieces, along with the pilot.

Whatever it was, they succeeded in assembling it quickly, set it on a swivel base, and aimed it toward the circling Cessna.

From shore, the captain gave the signal to commence shooting.

Just as the old plane was starting to swerve away, the first round of shots was fired, and missed.

It must be some poor fool who doesn't know what he's doing, Sommerville assumed, watching the Cessna. *He's got some grand, dated ideas about heroism and—*

For some moments it seemed the pilot had been scared off.

The gunner on the deck of the sub relaxed, joking with his crewmate, who was checking to see if the weapon needed to be reloaded.

"No need!" he boasted. "He's probably some old *Juden* swine! It's just like those cowards to run away and hide!"

Suddenly, after having gone a short distance north, the Cessna came back from an easterly direction, catching them by surprise.

The gunner didn't swing around fast enough.

As the plane swooped down for not more than a few seconds, the pilot dropped a grenade close to the two men, then soared nearly straight up, the engines audibly straining to execute this wrenching and dangerous maneuver.

I didn't think those planes could take such stress, Sommerville thought as he watched with increasing admiration. *Whoever the pilot is won't be able to avoid crashing if he keeps on doing stunts like that. The old joints in that kind of Cessna weren't built to withstand any kind of real battering, at least not like what he's giving them.*

The grenade exploded, throwing both men overboard, and extensively damaging the antiaircraft weapon they had used.

The captain roared with anger, his face a dark red. He ordered the men on the beach to fire at the plane as it was making another pass over the scene.

Again it was not hit.

"Bazooka!" he yelled in German. "Get it! Bring this imbecile down *now!"*

A bazooka had been brought on shore in the event the Germans ran into difficulty. It was now balanced on the shoulder of one of the crewmen and aimed toward the already returning Cessna, the men's low chatter revealing the amazement they felt over the pilot's stupidity, yes, but also his apparent bravery.

No! James Sommerville screamed silently as he watched. *No, you will not do this!*

He was crouched behind a sand dune just where the road ended and that strand of beach began.

Taking careful aim at the man holding the bazooka, he fired two shots from his Colt, both of them hits.

"What the h—?" roared the startled German captain as he spun around, distracted from the Cessna.

He saw the two members of the crew, one of them dead. The other was nearly so, coughing up great geysers of blood as his body momentarily twitched and jerked, then was still.

"Hit the beach!" the captain ordered.

The other men, including Benton Grantham, fell to their stomachs.

Behind them, the old plane seemed to be heading directly for the bridge that jutted up like an ancient castle tower from the middle of the sub.

"Stop him!" the captain yelled.

One of the Germans crawled toward another weapon hidden under a sand-covered piece of canvas.

As soon as the covering had been pulled off, Sommerville, squinting, was able to recognize it as a Guerlich twenty-millimeter gun that was classed as light artillery—a strange-looking weapon with a barrel that tapered from twenty-eight-millimeters at the breech to twenty-millimeters at the muzzle.

And it was heavy.

The one man frantically motioned for someone to tilt it upward so he could aim at the Cessna.

Sommerville had crawled to another position behind a second dune a couple of dozen feet to the left of the first one, this new spot giving him an angle to the right side of the prostrate men on the beach.

He jumped up, got off three shots, wasting one but with the others hitting the men struggling with the rather heavy Guerlich.

But, unlike earlier, this time someone spotted Sommerville's position.

"*There!*" the shout tore through the morning air.

A dozen rifles and pistols fired in his direction this time.

He was hit twice, one large-caliber bullet piercing his right shoulder, the second lodging in his side, its impact nearly tearing his arm off.

Wheeling with pain, he grabbed for the Tommy gun, stood with it in his other hand, the stock braced against his side, intending to retreat to the road. Ready with the machine gun to cut down anybody he saw, he tried to make it back to his car.

Sommerville staggered and fell, hearing the shouting voices of the Germans as they realized they had wounded him.

He knew he could not make it to the road. Blood had seeped out to his overcoat, and was spreading down the front.

He tightened his grip around the middle of the Tommy as he leaned back awkwardly against the sand.

"Good-bye, my dearest . . . ," Sommerville whispered hoarsely. "Tell our baby when he's old enough to understand that his old man died loving him even as a tiny spark of life inside his mother's body."

He heard movement behind him.

Apparently the crew of the U-boat had fanned out, taking no chances, and would attack him from at least two directions.

Footsteps.

And then a face peered over the sand dune in front of him.

His fingers tightened around the Tommy.

A shot was fired. But it didn't come from that weapon!

The figure only a few feet away yelled sharply and fell, hit in the temple.

Footsteps in back of him, so close now.

Sommerville managed to turn around and aim the Tommy in that direction.

He saw a man with a substantial gray beard holding a pitchfork in one hand and a rifle in the other.

"My hearing's not so good anymore," he said, smiling. "But, mister, I got a good eye; I sure proved that, didn't I?"

Sommerville groaned as he shifted himself slightly, no strength left for anything but that tentative turn, and saw more men, all older, fathers and grandfathers and others coming from any number of directions, converging from one end of that jetty-rimmed section of beach to the other. Their younger sons away on bloody battlefields east and west, they had only a grab-bag assortment of weapons, ranging from pitchforks and baseball bats to hunting rifles and a few ancient pistols. Draped over their stooped shoulders, some of them even carried large, quite cumbersome fishing nets with which they undoubtedly hoped to trap a German "barracuda" or two.

"Them Nazis're in *our* backyard now," the bearded one added. "We're gonna whip their butts real good!"

9

Casey Aldrich had glimpsed the tableau below. Someone behind a dune was firing at the intruders on the beach as they redeployed their small force, spreading out to provide more difficult, scattered targets. Entering a sharp angle, he had briefly pulled away, circling at a distance for a couple of minutes, then returned.

The Nazis were now running toward their raft. A fight ensued among them, and in a moment four seemed to have been left dead or wounded, their bodies in widening puddles of red against the white sand.

And then he saw the horde of men looking much like himself, older or slightly younger perhaps, more than a few of them out of shape. As he watched them he speculated that many of them undoubtedly were filled with the kind of regret and self-doubt that had choked him day after day over the past several years as newspaper and radio reports carried stirring stories of heroism and sacrifice, making a nation proud of those who were fighting the *krauts* and the *Japs.*

"But now the rest of us have a chance!" he exclaimed.

He had hoped there would be other planes joining him, like the one he was piloting. Those on the ground now, leading a charge, had gotten the message, but where were the other Cessnas? Was he being left to fight alone from the air?

Soon there was no choice, no more time to be spent killing time, nothing left to do but act on his own.

The German sailors were close to the sub, driven there by shots being fired at them from the beach. Return rounds came from two of them on the raft itself, which was now hit, air rapidly escaping, making it almost instantly no more than a limp piece of useless rubber.

The Nazis swam frantically behind the raft and managed to get up on the sub's deck before two of them were hit in the back, toppling over into the water.

The survivors raced up and over the sub's hull and onto the bridge, where the hatch was swung open and they started to scamper down inside.

They're going to do it! Aldrich thought. *They're going to—*

But there was no way he could allow that, absolutely no way.

He nosed the Cessna down, down, until sea spray misted the tiny windshield.

Only two Germans still had to get below. They both looked up, startled, as they heard the old plane coming toward them.

One of them raised a pistol at it, pulled the trigger, hit the propeller, then fired again, this time shattering the glass in front of him.

Just as Aldrich tried to swerve away, a huge water swell arose up, slapped at the front of the Cessna, and started to tip it over. The plane was slammed up against the side of the sub and partway onto its deck.

Both Germans hesitated, waiting for movement from the pilot. Then they burst into laughter, enjoying the fact that the attack had been aborted so conclusively.

"Hurry!" someone shouted from inside. "We dive now!"

One got down safely, still chuckling as he went, but as the other started to descend, he felt strong hands grab him and pull him back up.

"Go without me!" he shouted to his comrades below as he frantically grasped the ladder to keep from being dragged upward.

"No!" someone answered him. "We cannot! Your leg is in the way. We are unable to close the hatch unless we saw it off, Kurt! Hurry!"

The German struggled to break away from whoever held him from above but couldn't. He glimpsed for a moment the weathered face of Casey Aldrich, a cut on his forehead, several teeth missing.

After lashing out with a fist, forcing Aldrich to let go, the German was able to slide down into the U-boat.

"No!" Aldrich screamed, his bloodshot eyes widening as he leapt at the opening, getting half of his body, feet-first, through it before anyone tried to close the hatch.

Extending his right arm as straight as possible, he closed his fingers around the uppermost metal handgrip on the side of the bridge, then grasped a similar one on the underside of the hatch with his other hand, essentially locking both arms into place. Then he began kicking out with his heavy-booted feet as he felt hands wrapping around his legs and his hips as crew members attempted to yank him inside.

Aldrich heard someone shout, "The tide's going out. Kill the swine! We can feed him to the sharks later!"

Abrupt pain began in his lower torso as something sharp, he assumed it to be a knife, entered his stomach, followed by another piercing pain just below his left kidney, this one going through and emerging out his back.

"Dive! Dive!" he heard the same voice order, an edge of panic in the otherwise commanding tone.

"We are unable to do that, sir," another replied. "He's stuck in the hatch. We cannot close it!"

Aldrich had kicked so furiously that he momentarily beat back whoever was beneath him. Now, pain nearly causing him to lose consciousness, he further tightened both hands on the metal grips, hoping that in death this valiant grip, forged by years of working with heavy farm tools, would be frozen hard and immovable. Then the hatch could not be shut, with him blocking it as he was, and the U-boat would be incapable of diving deep into the Atlantic before the coming low tide stuck it quite helplessly in that little inlet.

"He will *not* be broken loose, Captain!" a desperate voice yelled.

"Then you had bloody well better amputate his arms at the shoulders or the wrists!" ordered another voice, deep and commanding.

Casey Aldrich died before they could cut into his body again but not before raising his head up toward the sky, he saw an aerial armada of Cessnas and other planes forming a large, sprawling umbrella of sorts above the U-boat, so many of them that the early-morning sun was blocked from his eyes as he closed them for the last time.

Stephen Bartlett and the other agents found that getting to James Sommerville took far longer than they had planned.

A middle-of-the-night accident on the main highway had resulted in a traffic tie-up that forced them onto side roads that led them once in the wrong direction and another time to the vigilance of a local police officer who demanded that they pull over their speeding car. When he discovered who they were and why they had been speeding, he suggested that he could help them connect with a shorter, less congested route, an offer Bartlett accepted, anxious to find Sommerville without further delay.

He tried to radio to the FBI agent half a dozen times.

No response . . . except for the final attempt.

He heard a voice at the other end, obviously someone not familiar with the operation of the radio.

Finally the connection was broken.

But not before the sound of gunfire crackled in the background.

Fifteen minutes later, he spotted the car Sommerville had used parked on a road paralleling the beach.

Bartlett slammed on the brakes of the Plymouth he had been driving and jumped out, signaling for the other men to follow, each of them carrying a rifle and a pistol. A few of them had sticks of dynamite protruding from behind their belts.

To their right were marshlike reeds interspersed among the white sand dunes.

They could hear vociferous, angry voices and the sound of many propellers slicing through the air.

Just ahead there was a flat section of that strand of beach where the view would be unobstructed.

They approached it with great caution.

Bartlett peered around the edge of a dune, then pulled back.

"What is it, sir?" a state policeman asked.

A look of astonishment had gripped Bartlett's face.

One by one the others walked past him onto the beach, then he joined them.

Stuck in the middle of an inlet created by two rock jetties on either side was a large, black U-boat.

Beyond it, blocking its exit, was a ragtag group—it could never be called a fleet—of fishing boats, rowboats, and inflated rafts; and beyond them, approaching the scene but not quite there yet, were half a dozen Coast Guard vessels of various tonnage.

Directly above, more than a dozen old planes hovered about the beach.

On the beach itself, middle-aged and older men holding pitchforks, rifles, scathes, baseball bats, and axes had surrounded the apparent crew of the sub.

To one side, Bartlett glimpsed four bodies; Benton Grantham's was one of them.

On a stretcher, being carried to an ambulance that had been driven onto the beach, was James Sommerville.

Bartlett rushed over to him before the rear doors were slammed shut.

A medic intercepted him.

"He's going to pull through, I think," he said, "but we have to get him to the hospital. He needs blood, a lot of blood, as soon as we can get it into him."

Bartlett flashed his identification.

"Do whatever needs to be done," he assured the medic. "This man has the full support of both the FBI and the OSS. The cost is unimportant!"

"We never worry about the money, sir. Saving lives is all that matters."

Bartlett nodded and waved him on.

Then he turned to the scene on the beach. State police and FBI agents had joined the group of middle-aged and older men ringing the crew of the U-boat.

Bartlett noticed that one of the prisoners was the captain.

"What is your name, Captain?" he asked in German as the others stepped aside to let him through.

"Helmutt Leinheiser," the other man replied curtly.

"Ah, your family comes from Leinhausen, a region of farmers and craftsmen, ropemakers, too, in the old days at least. They have been people of peace for centuries. How could someone with that kind of heritage serve a government dedicated to genocide?"

"You think me a Nazi?" Leinheiser spat out the words contemptuously. "I am a military man serving the Fatherland."

"But this nation of which you speak is drenched with the blood of—"

"Jews, yes! One does not have to be a Nazi to think of their kind with disgust!"

Bartlett paused, momentarily taken aback by that thought. Like most Americans, he, too, once had equated anti-Semitism strictly with members of the National Socialist Party. But when he was in Europe, he had detected flashes of resentment against the Jews even among the partisans. But he had never paid much attention to those feelings expressed by partisans since those very men, non-Jews that they were, fought for the liberation of their country from the architects of the Final Solution.

"You seem surprised that a *German* who has no love for the Nazis could feel as I do," Leinheiser commented.

Bartlett had to admit this was the case.

"It is possible to recognize how much harm they did to my country," the captain went on. "It is possible to hate them for that alone. But there is an even greater evil for which I shall blame them until the day I die."

"What is that, Captain Leinheiser?"

"They gave birth to the *need* for the madmen we now have at the power centers of my country. By handing over to the Nazis that very environment, which they could manipulate with such great skill, the *Juden* fostered destruction of the honor and the dignity and the decency of Germany for a very long time to come. They have made of us all grotesque phantoms of what we once were, disfigured and foul!"

Bartlett understood that no argument then would have any impact, so he started to walk away.

"I see that you are so confident that the United States and its allies have all but won this war," he could hear Leinheiser snarl after him. "But hear me well: That cannot be true. This I know. You will discover what that truth is very soon, for there remains only a matter of time before the Jews infesting the very fabric of *your* nation will find their cocoon-like security nonexistent for the rest of time!"

Bartlett turned around and did something that every instinct told him was wrong, that he had been trained specifically not to do, and for which he could be harshly reprimanded by William Casey and penalized in some other fashion as well.

It was a written rule in fact, very clearly stated.

The one about knocking a P.O.W. unconscious.

10

Stephen Bartlett intended to "mop up" and head on home, weary after a twenty-four period of nonstop crises.

But there was a delay, centered in the task of extricating Casey Aldrich's body from the sub where it had remained.

Coast Guard members had tried to break his hold on the hatch and the outside bar but they were unsuccessful. Fortunately, the crew of the vessel was able, one by one, to push past the body, though with the heftier ones, this proved quite a struggle.

And it resulted in a curious display of respect by one of them, a quite thin little man who had climbed up to the hatch and then stopped.

Casey Aldrich's head had been frozen into a profile position, and there was something of a smile on it.

The crew member reached out and brushed back some hair that had fallen over Aldrich's forehead.

"May God forgive us," he spoke sadly, "if somehow He can . . ."

Below, the others were yelling for him to move on.

He turned, looked down toward them, and added, "As you pass this brave man, remember what we all have caused this day and many more before it."

After the captain and the full crew of the U-boat had been taken ashore, only Casey Aldrich's body remained.

"We've tried everything," a Coast Guard crew member told Bartlett. "Oil won't work. I've never seen anything like this. It's almost as though he dared them to break him loose. And now we are the ones who have to do it."

"You have only one choice," he replied, his stomach rebelling at the prospect.

The other man's head bowed, unable to look at Bartlett.

One of the farmers, a burly giant of a man with pitch-black hair and thick, strong hands, overheard what was being said and approached them.

"My name is Len," he said, "Len Spedding . . . Casey Aldrich was a buddy of mine. I can help. I'll do it."

"You know what we're talking about?" Bartlett asked.

"Yes, I do."

He took out a long knife.

"It seems strange now, of course, but Casey gave this to me as a Christmas gift one year. It's the best blade around, very sharp and as strong as anything, but it's pretty thin and gives a clean cut, almost like a razor blade."

"I can't ask you to do this to a friend," Bartlett told him.

"Better that it be done by some stranger, is that what you're saying, mister?" Spedding shot back.

"I'll take you myself," Bartlett acquiesced.

Spedding's eyes clouded up.

"Sorry about my manner," he said. "Casey's dead now because he loved his country so much. That's kind of sad and beautiful all at the same time, don't you think?"

The body of Casey Aldrich hadn't blocked enough of the hatch opening to prevent the crew members from squeezing on through, but the position in which death had frozen him made closing the hatch impossible.

"It's really awful, I know, that we didn't get here before we did," Spedding said, his sorrow evident as they stood and looked at the pale, torn remains of Casey Aldrich. "But at least we made it before *they* cut him up anymore than they did."

Only that one foot had been severed from Aldrich's body.

He was stretched out in a position that resembled that of someone who had been crucified but tilted roughly forty-five degrees, his right arm dangling over the edge of the bridge, the fingers wrapped tightly around the metal grip on the outside of it.

His left hand was still jammed under the grip on the hatch itself, his head now leaning forward on his chest, his legs dangling like those of a puppet or doll abandoned in a small child's closet.

"He worried so much about being a worthy husband and father," Spedding remarked. "It haunted him, Mr. Bartlett."

He stood before the body, in the middle of the bridge, looking at the clean, silver-colored blade of the knife.

"The Coast Guard guys tried prying his fingers away," he said, "but lost any stomach for the job. They didn't want to snap his fingers like a twig from some old tree."

The mouth was hanging open, the lips twisted back.

"Can you imagine the pain?" he said. "It looks as though he cried out from it."

For a moment, Spedding closed his eyes, softly humming the melody of *Amazing Grace* and then abruptly he fell to his knees with a sob.

"I was in the Holy Lands before the war broke out," he murmured. "It was something I'd always wanted to do, to be where Christ had physically walked and healed and where He had died and . . . and—"

Spedding knew he was not making as much sense as he wanted to but he could not help himself.

His voice broke, and he had to clear his throat before he was able to continue: "Think of what the Lord endured. He was on that cross for hours. At least, with Casey here, I figure it was only minutes."

His hands went to his head.

"And the thorns!" he nearly shouted, tears gushing down the sides of his wrinkled and pockmarked cheeks.

"Spikes, too," added Bartlett, kneeling beside him, "and that centurion's spear in his side. Pain all over His body."

Spedding looked up at Casey Aldrich's bloodless face.

"My friend, my friend . . . ," Spedding added. "Casey was always there for me, but now I can do nothing for him."

They both were silent for a short while as each man prayed in his own separate way.

It was Spedding who stood first.

Despite his size, which exuded strength, he staggered a bit, and found himself leaning against Bartlett.

"Do you want me to do it?" Bartlett asked.

Spedding shook his head.

"No, it's got to be me . . . with Casey's own knife," he replied, not unkindly.

He walked the few inches to the hatch opening and examined the badly bruised wrist. Dried blood could be seen around the edges.

Spedding avoided looking at what was left of the stomach,

which had been lacerated by the murderers' punctures. Aldrich's jacket hung in shreds.

"His eyes, Mr. Bartlett," he said sadly. "They're still open . . ."

Spedding reached out, carefully closing the lids.

"Why didn't anybody from the Coast Guard do that before now?" he spoke. "What were those guys *thinking* of?"

In life Casey Aldrich was an inch or two shorter than Spedding, but stretching himself out as he had done meant that his friend now had to reach up to place the edge of the knife against his wrist.

"Would you be willing to wait in the raft?" Spedding asked.

"No problem," Bartlett told him.

"This is something between Casey and myself."

"I understand."

Bartlett climbed out of the bridge and walked across the deck to where the raft was attached to the sub by a heavy strand of rope.

As he was climbing into it he heard Len Spedding cry out, and he almost jumped back onto the sub but decided to wait so that the other man would be alone in that moment of grief.

Lord, I am feeling really weary, Bartlett prayed in silence. *Help me soon to get home to my loved ones. I want to hold them in my arms and feel their warmth before I witness any additional tragedies this day or any other. I need this very much, Lord.*

After a few minutes had passed, he could see Spedding jump over the edge of the bridge, Casey Aldrich's remains in a body bag they had brought with them.

The big man was smiling as he approached the little raft.

"I didn't have to do it!" he beamed. "Praise God, I didn't have to use the knife."

Bartlett was nonplused.

"How did you manage then?"

Spedding didn't answer right away, waiting until after they had gotten the body into the raft and pulled away from the sub.

"I really was going to do it, you know," he said when they had nearly reached the beach. "But I got to sobbing so bad—I mean, a big guy like me, there I was, like a baby, tears coming so fast that I could barely see. I thought I saw Casey's hand slide down from the hatch cover on its own, like he had somehow finally loosened his grip.

"I know how crazy that must sound but then it seemed to be happening with his right hand at the same time. I tried to tell myself that I was imagining things; you know, grief has a habit of doing crazy things to you, making your wishful thinking seem so real. But then . . . then—"

Spedding was shaking, every inch of his considerable frame reacting to the emotions that had taken hold.

"He slipped down, sir, just like that. Casey slipped down and fell against me. I . . . I didn't know what to do, I just reached out and put my arms around him and held him, like those times we'd go fishing and one of us would catch a big one, and we'd hug one another and . . . and—"

He took out the old knife from a sheath attached to his belt.

"I never had to touch poor Casey with this," he said, almost beside himself with joy. "I was praying so hard that the Lord *would* intervene and . . . and, you know, He surely did. I mean, how else could that have happened, sir? Nobody before we got here was able to *pry* my buddy loose!"

Some other explanations, Bartlett realized, could have come into play—after-death tremors of one sort or another were hardly unknown, providing the stuff of some memorably frightening moments for countless premed students over the years—but in the very coincidence of the timing of this particular episode rested the possibility that what Spedding had hinted was true.

As soon as they reached shore, the body was taken off the raft by several of Casey Aldrich's other friends. They placed it gently on the sand and formed a circle around it as they bowed their heads in silent prayer.

Four days later, there was a burial service at a small, old cemetery near Absecon, New Jersey, the community where Casey Aldrich had been born and raised. Three hundred people gathered, led by Aldrich's widow, Melanie, congesting the narrow roads in every direction.

Stephen Bartlett attended, along with top officials from the Civil Air Patrol. Aldrich's two sons didn't find out what had happened until mail finally got through to them nearly a month later as they were mopping up after helping to defeat fascist forces in Italy.

Only after the war ended were they able to visit the grave site and glimpse what was chiseled into the granite headstone: CASEY ALDRICH—1886–1944.

Both of the war-weary sons had seen the accumulated horrors of the battlefield across three countries and had learned as an act of survival to keep their emotions in check. But, just then, reaching out and holding one another for strength that chilly day in December, they read their father's epitaph, and could not contain the tears.

LET NO ONE BE ASHAMED OF HIM AS HUSBAND, FATHER, OR FRIEND, FOR THIS HIS LIFE WAS GIVEN FOR ALL

Part Two

11

James Sommerville's survival was uncertain for the first twenty-four hours after an emergency operation. He did pull through, but he would never again serve as an FBI agent in the field because of partial paralysis inflicted by his wounds. Responding in a show of compassion not unlike others he had carried out over the years, Hoover placed Sommerville on his personal staff at the bureau's headquarters.

One week later, at the time Bloody Winter *was supposedly due to commence, no offensive had been launched by the Nazi espionage network in concert with the ever-present U-boats off the East Coast and in the Gulf of Mexico.*

The expected offensive became a source of debate within the FBI and the OSS as Hoover and Casey, with input from Stephen Bartlett, tried to fathom what was going on . . .

Prematurely gray-haired William Casey was standing in front of a very large multicolored wall map in his office. A fully recovered J. Edgar Hoover sat in a comfortable old dark-brown padded chair at the OSS's United States headquarters, rubbing his eyes and groaning slightly.

Both men looked up as Stephen Bartlett entered.

"Terrible!" Hoover exclaimed. "It could not be worse, Stephen. The Nazis have reduced us to a waiting game while *they* control what happens next. It's very frustrating. They've taken the initiative right out of our hands."

"He's right," Casey agreed forlornly. "The back of the espionage apparatus was supposed to have been broken two years ago after Ignatz Griebl sang like a canary for six long, fruitful days, but we were wrong. Like weeds, they've been springing up everywhere. And now they've hit the Capitol."

Earlier, Dr. Ignatz Theodor Griebl had been an FBI success story. A respected surgeon and obstetrician, he was referred to in German espionage circles by the code name of *Ilberg*. His ranking was A.2339, which meant he was an active spy among the top echelon of such men and women.

Griebl and his associates were responsible for feeding to Berlin a massive amount of top-secret U.S. military data, including troop-strength specifications and blueprints for three navy destroyers, as well as devices that the Lear Radio Company was building for the U.S. Armed Services, a report on tactical air exercises at Mitchell Field, and various invaluable bits and pieces of information that were useful to the Germans.

Eventually he was tracked down and caught, only to escape and never again be found—but not before he unmasked a significant part of the Nazi spy-and-espionage apparatus in the United States!

Casey pointed to a folder on top of his desk. As Bartlett reached over and picked it up, Hoover groaned again.

"We could have done so much more before the war if our funding hadn't been cut by the mindless politicians on Capitol Hill and their bureaucratic flunkies!" he barked. "They'll slash money from where it's really needed and spend it on pork barrel projects to impress the voters back home! And in the meantime, the security of this nation goes down the drain."

In the manila folder were just two sheets of paper, with TOP SECRET stamped across the top of each.

"That's what my aide rushed over to me last Friday night near the restaurant, if you'll recall that moment," Casey said. "Good thinking on his part. It's as monumental as he guessed. My only regret is that you've not seen it before now. But I figured you needed a few days off with your family."

After thanking him, Bartlett sat down next to Hoover, reading the contents and learning more about *Bloody Winter*. Other than the chilling comment he had overhead on the night of the explosion he had been unaware of any up-to-date details.

Bloody Winter . . .

It apparently was the culmination of concentrated Nazi efforts to bring the United States to its knees and emasculate the Allied war effort.

"Nazi agents have managed to put together scores of meticulous maps dealing with *every major American city!*" exclaimed Bartlett as he read from the two sheets. "The details include actual blueprints of

New York City's water system. This is true as well of the Los Angeles water filtration plants and reservoirs."

"I think that was what happened at the restaurant," Hoover ventured, eager to appear more in command. "They used that situation as a test case."

Bartlett knew that the FBI director disliked being contradicted unless he specifically asked for contrary analyses.

"May I disagree, sir?" he asked somewhat tentatively.

"Go ahead, Stephen. Frankly it would not surprise me at all if *you* come up with a better answer."

Such compliments from Hoover were hardly common.

"Thank you, sir," he replied. "As you know, I overheard something at the German Embassy before everything went haywire."

Too much chaos too early in the game. Your actions may backfire . . . do you not realize that we have given them that very week to act on suspicions that are certain to be generated?

"Overzealous 'patriots' who should have been given a shorter leash?" Casey asked. "Is that what you're suggesting, Stephen?"

"I think so. But I'd like to go over the rest of this material you've given me before I say anything else."

Casey nodded in agreement, and Bartlett continued reading the top secret report.

"You must be at the paragraph about the Horseshoe Curve of the Pennsylvania Railroad near Altoona and the Hell Gate Bridge over the East River in New York City," Casey spoke as he saw the other man's eyes open wide. "But it won't be ending with those. Dozens more targets of sabotage may be involved. And all happen to be *civilian* in orientation. You will find no military bases listed in that communiqué."

He reached into the center drawer of his desk, pulled out an additional sheet and handed it to Bartlett.

"On the other hand, we have to look at another possibility, that it's not sabotage after all and will be an overt military attack launched by camouflaged U-boats with an arsenal of *Vergeltungswaffen!*" Bartlett blurted out as he began reading the additional information. "Every one of these could be aimed at our most crucial bases, the civilian targets acting only as diversions for the military attacks."

The *Vergeltungswaffen,* or V-1s, were the infamous buzz bombs that the Nazis had started to send against London and other English locales four months earlier—essentially pilotless aircraft with speeds reaching more than four hundred miles per hour. When they entered the air space above their target, a timing device shut off the engine and sent the bombs plummeting. The resulting explosion delivered two tons of fury, killing nearly six thousand British men, women, and children, injuring more than forty thousand others, and damaging or totally destroying in excess of seventy-five homes as well as offices and other buildings, many of these of irreplaceable historical value.

All of this happened despite the fact that Hawker Tempest fighter planes were able to intercept and explode as many as 630 of the V-1s!

Bartlett acted as though someone had hit him with a well-aimed boxing glove.

"Wait a minute!" he exclaimed as he sprang forward in his chair, asking, with sudden suspicion, "sir, I am wondering if you would enlighten me as to how all this information came into our hands in the first place?"

Casey slammed his fists down on the top of his desk.

"That is *exactly* the point, Stephen. I'm not surprised that you were able to pick up on it. You might say that every bit of it was *handed* to us by one of the spies we captured last week in a raid, a woman from Brooklyn, New York. She was posing as an everyday housewife. Her name is Lilly Barbara Stein.

"There is some reason to believe that, because she isn't a pure Aryan, she was blackmailed into cooperating with the underground Nazis in this country and forced to take up training at Klopstock Pension, a secret espionage school near the National Socialists' head-quarters in Hamburg."

"So, this Stein woman may not have been completely loyal to the *Führer* then," Bartlett surmised.

"That's what we suspected at the time. Nevertheless, she seemed to give in all too easily when she was captured by our men. At the time, they were counting themselves fortunate indeed, without seriously doubting her motives. I never thought anything of this until now, chalking it up to our expertise at interrogation."

Bartlett sat up straight in his chair.

"Could it be that the Nazis are deliberately trying to confuse us?" he posed to the other two men.

"What would *that* accomplish?" Casey asked, though he already knew the answer and only wanted Bartlett to show his stuff before Hoover because of the implicit competition that often reared up between the two departments.

"They hope it would cause us to squander our efforts by covering *all* the military bases *as well as* the probable civilian targets," Bartlett suggested. "In their eyes, this only ensures that we're destined to become sloppy somewhere sometime. *Any* mistake we make, especially now, is a plus for National Socialism."

Hoover loudly cleared his throat, his customary way of breaking into the middle of a conversation. As pompous as he sometimes seemed, he was nevertheless a man of special ability in a number of respects, and both Casey and Bartlett had learned to hold off any skepticism until he had offered what was on his mind, since the FBI director usually came alive in a crisis situation. And no one doubted the crisis pitch of the present dilemma! It was only when Hoover had no excitement to occupy his time that his fundamental shortcomings took over, causing him to periodically make a fool of himself, at least in the eyes of his many critics.

"Are we perhaps on the wrong track here?" Casey asked in what seemed an almost flippant tone.

Hoover shook his head.

"What you are conjecturing sounds reasonable," he said, his eyes darting from side to side, a trait that showed his mind was racing over a variety of possibilities until he could settle upon one that he considered the most likely. "I might even point out that what you have been saying is exactly how we should be *expected* to react."

"I'm glad you agree," Casey said jubilantly, not quite catching what the other man had insinuated. "We'll need to act accordingly."

Hoover raised his left hand, rather like a student in school trying to attract a teacher's attention. With other men, he would have jumped to his feet and taken center stage. But he respected Casey more than most.

"You misunderstood my comment," he spoke. "I am thinking of something altogether different. What we just might have here is a brilliant con game to divert our attention from their *real* plans. While we are congratulating ourselves on our powers of discernment, our enemy may be preparing for the last laugh.

"Explain . . . ," Casey requested, twirling a pencil between his fingers as he enjoyed seeing a man often ridiculed in Congress and by the media show the side of his personality that his critics conveniently ignored.

"If we become convinced that they are trying to trick us with a dummy mission aimed at our military bases, as you said, and therefore choose to ignore that supposedly fake threat in order to concentrate on the civilian targets, which we assume are the *authentic* ones . . ."

Hoover paused, for effect, then added, "what *about* those bases, I must ask, gentlemen? Other than the normal safeguards present in this wartime environment of ours, which would be little protection against an attack from the sea, they would be ripe for attack by a remote-control enemy sending pilotless aircraft. Hundreds of them are probably being readied from such a vast number of locations that we could not counter all of them. *Some would get through!*"

Casey snapped the pencil in half as he grasped what the FBI director was postulating.

"It is entirely possible that the Nazis want us to believe that this report *has* been deliberately planted by their operatives," he exclaimed, "and, therefore, is nothing more than a decoy. *The old cry-wolf syndrome!*"

Now Hoover stood and walked slowly over to a mammoth wall map of the United States that hung beside maps of the European and Pacific war theaters. He stood there, briefly studying it and reflexively scratching his right cheek.

"This is so serious," he spoke after a minute or two, "that we have to keep as much information from the general public as we can manage. It is doubtful that they would cope well with any idea of having to face dual lines of attack, from espionage cadres on land as well as a fleet of U-boats firing their unholy weapons from the Atlantic and the Gulf of Mexico."

"So we have no idea of when this will happen," Bartlett interjected. "What I overheard at the embassy was obviously false. Since they couldn't have known I was there, listening, it must be that even their own spies are being fed false information so that, if captured, they cannot divulge the truth!"

"Not knowing when it will come is the worst possible state for us to be in," Hoover told them both. "We simply do not have enough manpower to safeguard every possible target. So close to their own defeat, Hitler and his henchmen may have hit upon the one plan to slow us down!"

He was thinking of how easily German craft had gotten into the Caribbean as well as the Gulf of Mexico, where they had sunk sixty-nine vessels from various ports, fully a third of the ships destroyed worldwide by the Germans, causing Admiral Karl Doenitz to brag, "German submarines are operating so close to shore along the American coast that sunbathers and sometimes whole cities are witnesses to that drama of war whose visual climaxes are the red glorioles of blazing tankers."

Hoover sighed as he recalled the relieved mood throughout the United States when these attacks had seemed to subside a few months earlier.

"How foolish we were!" he spoke. "We thought the enemy had given up naval offenses altogether after our ships in the Atlantic and the Mediterranean began to take such a heavy toll on their submarines. In addition, we began to hit brutally hard with air raids on their shipyards and their U-boat pens."

"Agreed," Casey put in. "But the Germans never did stop their building program; they just ceased deploying the vessels and shifted many of them into hiding, all of which lulled us into assuming we had gained the upper hand! Yet, just this month, reports finally indicate the truth—that the German government has continued turning out U-boats, in fact, more during the past six months than at any other time in this war! Now we have some indication of why they've been doing this."

Without warning, Hoover clapped his hands together, startling Casey and Bartlett.

"Listen to me!" he told them abruptly. "We face the potential of Armageddon at any moment! It is little wonder that some well-meaning people have thought that Hitler might be anti-Christ. We all know that he isn't, but who can blame the uninformed for thinking that?"

Hoover looked at them both with an expression at once curiously intent and also unusually warm.

"At present we have but one source of genuine help," he continued. "It means that we must get on our knees before almighty God and ask for guidance, protection, and just a measure of His eternal wisdom."

Both Bartlett and Casey were surprised, but they didn't hesitate to do as Hoover asked, knowing that it was a rare moment and might never again occur for the three of them. On that particular November morning, less than a year before the end of World War II, J. Edgar Hoover, William Casey, and Stephen Bartlett knelt together, joining hands, and praying as none of them had ever done before.

Afterward, as Hoover was about to exit Casey's office, he turned, biting his lower lip, and said, "Gentlemen, in view of what we have just prayed, I am reluctant to tell you something else, a likelihood that has arisen just within the past twenty-four hours."

Another Hoover characteristic involved stage-managing as much of any important meeting as possible, and one favorite ploy was to pretend the meeting was over and he was in the process of leaving, only to spring perhaps the most important revelation of all on the other participants.

"Yes?" Casey said, aware of the other man's little games but no longer turned off by them since he had to admit that Hoover's innate brilliance was worth the sometimes childish displays of manipulation.

"I must tell you the circumstances with the understanding that *nothing* goes beyond this office," Hoover said sternly as he placed the palms of his hands on the back of the chair in which he had been sitting. "Can I count on this?"

Casey and Bartlett assured him that he could.

"A longshoremen's strike is scheduled for the New York harbor area in two days!" he declared.

"Just as we're turning the tide of the war?" Casey blurted out. "We cannot have an interruption in supplies or materiel. The enemy's supply line is being shattered on a daily basis. Until now ours has been pretty much untouched. We cannot continue hammering the Germans nonstop if those stupid—"

He knew his temper was volcanic and that he had to control it for the sake of his health, but the sheer idiocy of such a stoppage at precisely the worst time was more than he could tolerate without showing what he felt.

"If it's not the Communists with these guys, it's the fascists!" he bellowed.

"But we need them, as you have said," Hoover went on.

"Yes, yes, that's the sad fact of life with which we are faced. What can you do, my friend? What can you do?"

"It will be controversial, I warn you."

"Any more so than losing the war just when we appear to be winning it?"

"To some in this country, especially that self-satisfied, arrogant crowd at Hyannis Port, the answer isn't what you might suspect," Hoover admitted. "They're so sheltered, they think, behind all that wealth, that the Nazis will be no problem nor will their own government, no matter how many near-treasonous actions they take or statements they make. I wonder how the old man can think the way he does while his own sons are—"

Hoover's face had become dark red. He cut himself off and struggled to keep his feelings in check.

"Agreed," Casey said, realizing that even now the other man needed just a little bit of coaxing. "We're listening. What do you have in mind?"

"Stephen now has had direct contact with Benedetto Vincenzo Santapaola," Hoover reminded them. "I think some 'persuasion' from his men would get the longshoremen to change their minds with rather startling speed."

Getting into bed with mobsters could never be in the best interests of the country because, whether stated or not, the mafioso would expect some concessions later on to pay them back for their efforts. Yet the situation within the United States had become desperate now, as well as during the years when the infestation of spies had been at its greatest level. Before, Hoover had told his agents to look the other way whenever possible if they encountered a mafia "situation," a dictum that Christopher Lyons had chosen to ignore. This was in return for the FBI's being tipped off about espionage activity by the mafioso families.

But, always, direct contact with Santapaola, perhaps the most powerful of all the dons, had proved elusive. Oldest survivor of the Prohibition gangland wars, he had learned to hate the Feds when he was one of Al Capone's inner circle. Not even Meyer Lanski, who later would prove instrumental in gaining support for the establishment of a Jewish state in Palestine, could convince Santapaola to cooperate, so embittered was the old man.

"I will *never* consort with the murderers of my friends," he bellowed on one occasion, "no matter what government they claim as their own. They drove Capone into the grave, and he is not the only one. *I spit in the face of Hoover and his self-righteous band of thugs!*"

But with Stephen Bartlett, it might prove another story.

"Thank God we don't have to worry about the Teamsters as well," Casey commented sardonically.

The kind of persuasion Hoover mentioned involved verbal intimidation, physical injury, and possibly a death or two in order to get the mob's point across. Not even the tough dockside workers would be able to stand up against what Benedetto Vincenzo Santapaola was capable of throwing at them.

Bartlett's palms became sweaty.

"Do you want me to sound him out?" he asked uncomfortably, sensing that they were about to ask.

Hoover stood without speaking but not in a posturing manner this time. He was obviously experiencing some turmoil about the implications.

"Would you agree that Stephen should?" he asked of Casey, both of them with anguished expressions.

Casey looked at Bartlett, then back to Hoover, and finally up at the ceiling.

"We've done it before," he said, the admission not a comfortable one for him.

"Where?" Bartlett asked, unprepared for that.

"In Italy, Stephen . . . the Sicilians have been very helpful to us there. Many of them showed considerable courage as they stood up to Mussolini."

Bartlett realized he had been kept in the dark about this but decided not to challenge Casey in front of Hoover.

As it turned out, he didn't need to.

"The less any one man in the field knows about other operations, the better off we all are," Casey told him with little elaboration. *"As it is, Stephen, you have been privy to more insights about various aspects of our theater of operations than any other agent with the OSS. This couldn't be helped."*

Bartlett sensed the truth of that. It seemed premeditated and a bit callous but also necessary to safeguard the activities of a network of other agents. Letting one man know more than he should made that individual a potential target for Nazi interrogators eager to unravel the Allied counter-espionage effort.

"Thank you for telling me," he said, genuinely grateful.

Hoover spoke up then.

"Stephen, you're a Christian. Will this be a problem for you?"

Bartlett wished Hoover hadn't raised that issue.

"I seem to recall a verse from the Bible that says light shall not have fellowship with darkness," the FBI director added. "Won't you be transgressing that one admonition and possibly others?"

Bartlett was surprised by Hoover's reference to Scripture.

"This whole war is essentially about light and darkness clashing," he replied. "That's by far the greater issue, sir. We're told not to *kill* another human being, for example, and certainly no commandment is better known than that one. But the original language suggests that *murder* is a more apt translation than *kill*, and that God never intended to exclude such acts as those of authentic self-defense."

He could see that both men were listening intently.

"As I see it, we *are* fighting for our survival," Bartlett added. "I serve a *righteous* cause here as a result. I assure you that I could not do otherwise."

"Does that cover it then?" Hoover probed.

"I believe so, sir."

Hoover got to his feet.

"Enough of this!" he proclaimed. "Stephen, do you have wheels, as they say?"

Bartlett acknowledged that he did not.

"I took a taxi," he replied. "My wife has the car."

Bartlett glanced at him. There was obviously something on the man's mind.

"I shall take you then."

Bartlett glanced for a moment at Hoover, a man who had always seemed a bit sad behind that facade of bull-dog toughness. If any other individual had been involved, a dinner could have been easily arranged some days later—Natalie would have enjoyed preparing something for such a man—but because of Hoover's position, it would not have seemed proper for an OSS *agent*, however noted he may have been, to invite the renowned head of the FBI to his house. Hoover tended to spend his time with men of power such as the president of the United States, various members of Congress, and influential business leaders.

The three of them walked out together, heading for the parking garage under the building where the OSS had been maintaining its American headquarters. Bartlett was surprised that Hoover had no driver waiting beside the car the bureau provided for its director.

"I like to drive myself sometimes," Hoover replied with a shrug when he noticed Bartlett's surprise.

"Well, are you sure about this, sir? I can get a cab," Bartlett offered.

"At this hour, on a Saturday? *That* would be difficult," Hoover said humorlessly.

He was inserting the key in the ignition when the lights in the garage went out. They heard Casey yell suddenly, then the sound of gunfire followed by a door slamming shut.

12

The whereabouts of the inner sanctum of the OSS was supposed to be known only to a select group of individuals limited to the president of the United States, the vice-president, as well as William Casey and J. Edgar Hoover and, it was said, the secretaries of state and defense. In fact, the location in the nation's capital was moved periodically in order to safeguard it from any possible retaliation engineered by Wilhelm Canaris and his network of master spies and saboteurs, men and women with an astounding individual and collective ability to dig out secrets that would have failed discovery by even the best Allied spies.

When Canaris was implicated in the July 1944 plot to assassinate Hitler at Rastenburg, Germany, the Allies sighed with relief because they correctly assumed that no one else could operate as effectively as Canaris had proven was the case with himself. What no one had counted on, though, was a sense of desperation taking over among the Nazis and caution being replaced by wild acts of covert aggression.

The darkness in the garage was near total as both Bartlett and Hoover pulled their Colts.

Casey had been parked at the opposite end.

"Sir?" Bartlett asked.

"Yes . . . ," Hoover said, his voice strained.

"Wait here, please."

The FBI director agreed.

There were half a dozen other cars in the garage. Most undoubtedly had been left there overnight for whatever reason.

Bartlett made it to Casey's car without interference.

The OSS director was on the floor, trying to pull himself up. Dangling over the running board was the radio microphone.

"We'll have help in minutes," he groaned, pointing to it.

"Are you shot?" Bartlett asked after helping him to his feet.

"No, just socked with something very hard. I was the one who did the shooting."

"Did you see what they looked like?"

"I didn't—just that there were three of them. They headed upstairs. I suspect they would have preferred going for the exit and making it to the street, but you and Hoover were close enough to have gotten in their way."

"How did they find out where we were located?"

"It's impossible to say, at least for the moment."

Bartlett wasn't sure how to respond to that, and he said so. He wasn't able to keep his growing apprehension hidden because the implications included the potential of a supremely dangerous secrecy leak.

"I mean, this building is quite large, as you have seen," Casey clarified, "and it houses much more than just our little portion of it. Even the FBI has some top secret auxiliary offices here. Scores of people come and go daily. Such sheer numbers represent an enormous potential for leaks, don't you think? I argued against a structure of this sort, preferring a smaller, more secluded building, one we could more easily control, especially anyone entering or leaving it. But what we all are facing is something that tends to cripple us all, a restrictive budget that is in part manipulated by isolationists who refuse to loosen their death grip on us!"

Casey was right, raising the possibility that whatever the intruders had in mind could have been directed at more than one target inside the building.

"Any impression that you caught them in time, sir?" Bartlett asked.

"No way of knowing that, either, Stephen, except that they *seemed* to be leaving, not just caught as they were entering. But that's not definitive. I can't be sure."

"If so, then they must have arrived here in the garage barely seconds ahead of us, cut off the electricity, and hidden while we were getting into the cars."

"That's what I suspect. Obviously they didn't use the elevator, or we would have noticed the activity."

"I'm going inside, sir."

"No!" Casey insisted.

"I agree!" Hoover's voice interpolated itself.

He had come up behind them and had overheard the last bit of conversation.

"You're too valuable," Hoover added. "Without electricity you'll have no lights, and it's a maze up there. It would be impossible to find anybody."

Their admiration was flattering, but Bartlett would have preferred not being tied down by the concerns it generated.

"How long were we in the office?" Bartlett asked, a trace of impatience in his voice. "About an hour perhaps?"

"Possibly a little more than that," Casey agreed. "What are you getting at?"

"They were here, outside the building, when we arrived, and they snuck in right behind us. We saved them a break-in that might have set off some alarms they probably knew nothing about. And they were waiting, again, just now. But something went wrong. They got careless, it seems. They couldn't get past the gate at the entrance because we hadn't opened it yet. They had no choice but to go back upstairs."

"And that's why they collided with me!" Casey exclaimed. "They probably panicked, then out the window went their carelessly hatched plan of action."

"And also, they missed an opportunity to get rid of the three of us that had been handed to them by pure chance," Bartlett suggested.

Hoover and Casey glanced at one another.

"A moment ago," Bartlett added as he turned to Casey, "you said you had the impression that they were *leaving*, not entering. I think you're right, sir. Which may indicate that, whatever they hoped to do, they've already accomplished. They tried to sneak out of here and not be noticed. As it stands, their mission borders on being a failure since we've obviously been alerted to the fact that *something's* going on!"

"Bombs? Is that it?" spoke up Hoover, claustrophobia nibbling at him in the confines of the garage, edged as it was with the uncertainty of what the saboteurs had intended. "Could they have planted a series of bombs in critical spots throughout this building set to go off at a time only they know?"

"Or they could have put something in the water, sir, as they did at the restaurant, though that is less likely given the sheer size of this structure."

Hoover's mouth dropped open.

"If they were at the restaurant, and now they're here, then where else tomorrow or later?" he muttered. "We've been assuming, before this moment, that they were intending just one target as an example. What if the entire city is being set up in this manner?"

The four-story building was soon surrounded by dozens of federal officers, as well as other men serving the Washington, D.C., police department and half a dozen fire trucks with nearly twenty firemen ready.

"They've got to be still in the building," Police Chief Clarence Atkins commented. "Look at the front entrance."

The specially reinforced door was intact, with no evidence of anything broken or forced open at the lock or the hinges.

"And it's unlikely they could have gotten a key," he said, "unless someone inside is a double-agent."

"If that were so, they would have been long gone," Bartlett spoke up, "with no need to wait in the garage."

Chief Atkins seemed a little flustered by the presence of such celebrated "heavyweights" as William Casey and J. Edgar Hoover, though physically he was bigger than either of them and had actually been in law enforcement longer.

"Do you want to enter now?" he asked, holding up the key that the building's manager had provided.

Hoover looked around him at the FBI agents who were waiting for whatever his orders happened to be, his gaze seeming to be on every last one of them with nobody daring to look away from him.

Over the years, the veterans among them had learned to love or hate this man, often both, but none of them had anything but respect for him. He proved himself capable of what seemed to be a callous attitude that carried with it hints of cruelty if certain agents did not *exactly* carry out his instructions, but when news of this leaked to outsiders he was quick to defend himself as interested in one objective, and only that.

"This army shall have but one commander," he would say. "Anything else invites an appalling degree of success by the enemy."

So Hoover became more and more a dictator over the years, allegedly seeking headlines as much as any success against organized crime in various forms that the Federal Bureau of Investigation was supposed to be combating. His actions were influenced, according to his critics, by ego and plain mean-spiritedness mixed with paranoia.

And yet stories about Hoover's moments of pure kindness did seem even more plentiful than those of his maddeningly cold-hearted indifference, including telephone calls made by him to the grieving widows of agents killed during the performance of their duties but these were somewhat rare in comparison to the *visits* he made, at his own expense, a curious blend of personal caring and bottom-line bullheadedness. He would sit for hours with widows and with sons, daughters, sisters, brothers, sobbing along with them.

The latest situation was one in which J. Edgar Hoover excelled—being unquestionably in command of more than three dozen crack FBI agents—brave, intelligent, and resourceful men, principally in their thirties or early forties, who nevertheless couldn't make a move without being told what to do by the man to whom they had pledged an allegiance second only to that of the United States itself.

"Go in as planned," he instructed them in his patented staccato manner that bore some comparison to actor James Cagney. "Do not hesitate to shoot whenever necessary. No one else is authorized to be in there. *Anyone* you happen to meet up with is, therefore, highly suspect."

Abruptly he turned to Stephen Bartlett.

"You're as accustomed to their type of criminal mind as anyone here," he admitted. "Would you be willing to join my men? Can you do this, Stephen? You *do* have the right to refuse."

Bartlett was surprised.

"Sir, I would be happy to go," he said, his pulse quickening.

"Your director and I didn't want you challenging the saboteurs alone. But now you will have more than forty of the bureau's top men with you. There's no way they can succeed against such a group."

Bartlett nodded appreciatively.

"I hope I am worth your confidence in me," he replied.

Hoover turned to the others.

"Bartlett here is one of you in this operation," he told the others. "Heed any advice he might have. He's been with scum like this on their native soil! None of us has. That makes him an invaluable asset."

The gathered agents murmured enthusiastic agreement, a stark contrast to the attitude shown by Christopher Lyons earlier.

Chief Atkins inserted the key into the lock on the front door and stepped aside. Forty-five men filed past him into the four-story building with little idea of what they would be encountering over the coming minutes.

The hunt had begun.

13

No intruders were found on the ground floor.

Nor was there any real hint that anyone except the agents themselves had entered the various offices since employees had left for the weekend.

Before beginning the operation, Hoover personally contacted the heads of the various agencies and departments occupying space inside, and an official with a high security clearance from each was dispatched to accompany the agents.

One by one, they inspected the various suites. One by one they gave the same pronouncement, adding to the frustration of the FBI agents.

"There's no indication that anyone's been here since the building was closed for the weekend," one observed. "Yet it is this very floor that has the bulk of the high-security offices and files. It's almost as though they ignored it altogether and went elsewhere. But that's just plain stupid!"

The agent stood in the middle of the main corridor, genuinely puzzled that there was no success in uncovering the slightest clues, then he grunted and went back inside a nearby office.

Nearly fifteen minutes passed.

The report was the same from the second floor.

"Nothing!" a younger agent, who had identified himself as Jack Hibbert, remarked. "I can't believe that they spent some time here, yet seem to have done nothing."

"Surely this would be the place where they'd want to do *something*," Bartlett said. "I'm surprised that they were able to find out about it, but once they did, they surely must have considered it a cornucopia of sorts!"

They were standing in a satellite state department office.

"Some of the country's most sensitive data are right here," he went on. "What in the world were they thinking of by *not* touching anything?"

Bartlett noticed a long scar on Hibbert's left cheek and asked about it.

"It happened during the closing days of Prohibition," he answered matter-of-factly. "I was helping Elliott Ness. One of Capone's henchmen got to me. I was left in a ditch somewhere . . . almost bled to death."

Memories of that time in Hibbert's life seemed to be playing out in his eyes, pain reflected in them.

"It was very cold that night, Stephen, and I was getting weaker and weaker, " he spoke. "I have never felt as completely without hope as I did then. Cars went by. Some of the drivers slowed down, looking at me, then they went right on their way, not wanting to get involved, particularly in an era where mob 'executions' were appallingly common."

"Who stopped finally?" Bartlett asked.

"A Baptist minister. It was like something right out of the New Testament, Stephen. The others saw me, sure enough they did, probably even felt some pity for me, but they drove on without doing anything to help. But that one man, that wonderful—"

He wiped his eyes with the back of his hand.

The walkie-talkie Hibbert was holding in his other hand suddenly started spouting what seemed like gibberish at first.

"I can't make out what you're saying," he said. "Talk a little more slowly."

Noise—coughing—came over the radio, and what sounded like chairs being overturned. Someone was screaming . . . then coughing violently.

"Upstairs!" he yelled.

The stairwell was down the corridor to their right. As they started up the flight, the metal steps under their feet shook suddenly.

Both men took out their Colts before they made it up to the second floor.

As Hibbert was opening the door, they heard the sounds of confusion inside and an overpowering odor.

Hydrocyanic gas!

The same deadly substance used to dispose of prisoners at the Nazi death camps.

Agents were stumbling into one another. Some were already on the floor, coughing up great puddles of blood. Among them were the officials and others Hoover had summoned. All seemed very close to dying.

"The ventilation system!" someone yelled. "They're doing it through the ducts. We have to get out of here!"

There was the sound of windows breaking as chairs were thrown through the panes to get fresh air inside.

Some men did not think only of themselves but dragged other agents along with them, trying to reach the windows, but some not making it as they and those they were attempting to help fell on top of one another.

"They're dying," Hibbert said as he started to bolt inside. "We've got to—"

Bartlett pulled him back and slammed the door behind him.

"Outside, Jack!" Bartlett replied. "The saboteurs must be on the next floor. Undoubtedly, they sent down through the ducts some kind of explosive device with the gas canister, or whatever poison they used, attached to it."

"Spreading the gas throughout this floor!"

"But no farther than that. The stuff has little reach. And it dissipates quickly. They didn't pick street level because it would have been easier for our guys to get out by breaking through the front door and making it to the street."

Hibbert still held on to the door knob.

"Don't do it! Let go, Jack. A typical Nazi undercover agent has been trained as well as any of us. Get help outside! That's the best thing you can do for the men in there. Any of the fire departments here by now will have brought along some masks. Tell them to send out an emergency call for others. *Hurry!*"

Hibbert nodded, calming himself as much as he could, and hurried back down the stairs.

Beyond the door, Bartlett heard men dying.

He had to steel himself to avoid jumping into what he had just cautioned another man against doing. As he turned away, one of the agents flung the door open and stumbled toward the steps leading to the ground floor.

Bartlett raced toward him, but couldn't grab him in time. The man's blood-red eyes were bulging as he fell backward and tumbled down the flight of stairs, painfully hitting each step. He slammed hard against the concrete floor at the bottom and bounced grotesquely like a piece of fruit become overripe by excessive exposure to the sun.

He shrieked as the agony intensified throughout his body.

Then, his body devastated by the cumulative effects of the gas, blood seemed to cover the agent in a pathetic and grisly flood, the normal circulation in his veins and arteries backing up and gushing forth through the pores of his skin.

Bartlett took two steps at a time to reach him but he needn't have bothered. Death came in the next instant as the man's heart collapsed, along with his lungs and kidneys, unable to withstand the shock.

Enraged, Stephen Bartlett run back up the stairs and on to the third floor.

As soon as he had reached it and opened the entry door, he heard voices. These had no hint of accent and seemed young.

Are they recruiting kids now? he asked himself, *from the Hitler Youth Corps?*

One of them was crying.

"I didn't think it would *be* like this!" the young speaker whined. "We were supposed to be able to get in, plant everything, and leave without anybody seeing us."

A hint of a struggle, then—

"Quiet!" the first voice cautioned. "Dad's coming back."

Dad!

Apparently a father was involved along with his two sons!

Bartlett felt nauseous.

An older, gruffer voice could now be heard, confirming his suspicions.

"It's all set, guys," he told them, pride evident in the tone of his voice. "You both did a great job."

"But how do we get out?" one of his sons asked, his voice trembling.

"We don't," their father declared coldly.

"What do you mean, Dad?" both of his sons spoke at once.

"We can't allow the authorities to apprehend us now. We know far too much. All of us must be dead before they figure out where we are."

Bartlett heard one of the two young men gasp and apparently stumble back and trip over something as he backed away.

"*Dad! Don't!*" both shouted at the same time.

One shot . . . then another.

Bartlett threw the door open and dropped to his stomach in the corridor just inside, his teeth jarring as he hit the hard floor.

A third shot, this one lodging in the wall behind him.

He raised his head slightly and saw what was left of a pebbled glass partition a few feet in front of him. Beyond the shattered partition a man stood between two desks, the adding machines turned over, papers strewn in several directions, and a window directly in back of him. He held a pistol in both hands, and he was aiming at the prostrate intruder.

Bartlett rolled over, instantly swinging his own handgun up, and pulled the trigger four times in rapid succession before the other man could fire again.

One bullet missed, shattering the pane behind the other man. The second caught him in his left arm, just above the elbow, flinging it backward like the broken limb of a lifeless mannequin. The third grazed his right ear, loping part of it off, while the fourth ripped through his left hand, taking the better part of two fingers with it.

He staggered back, the gun falling to the debris-littered floor.

Bartlett jumped up, shouting, "Why the two of *them?*" Why did you do this? They're just kids! You gave them life!"

"I didn't want my sons to grow up in a world dominated by a bunch of Jew scum!" the man shouted, his face contorted with rage as well as pain. "That would have been worse than death for any true Aryan."

Bartlett walked slowly toward him. The man backed away with each step.

"But what have you accomplished here? You've been stopped before you could complete your mission. Isn't that much obvious? You *failed,* and you're not able to face that."

The man, bald, his head coming nearly to a point at the back, his eyebrows large, bushy, little flecks of fresh blood dotting his Hitlerian mustache, roared with laughter that shook his substantial frame.

"You think that is it, you Jew-loving idiot? I am not an American corrupted by Nazi dogma. I am a patriotic German liberated by the *Führer*'s vision of greatness, and I am now merely *posing* as an American.

"There are many of us in this country, you know. You didn't get *everyone* when you captured Ignatz Griebl. You found only the very tip of the iceberg. This country of yours is nothing more than the S.S. *Titanic,* and you are sinking whether you and your crippled president and your other Jew lackeys realize it or not.

"My comrades and I are among you everywhere, living next door, delivering your mail, walking the halls of Congress, teaching your children. You'll never find *all* of us, for that would be impossible even if you end up winning this war. We blend in far too well. We are your friends, your co-workers, your bankers, your grocery clerks!"

He was right up against the window frame, which gaped empty except for the jagged pieces of glass now sticking out of it.

"We *know* about *Bloody Winter,*" Bartlett yelled. "There are no surprises left. We *will* stop this madness of yours."

"Is that what you think, Stephen Bartlett?" the man said, smirking, as color drained from his face.

Bartlett tried not to show any surprise at the mention of his name.

"You don't want me to know how much it startles you that I, a stranger, am aware of who you are, do you?" the other man continued. "But I can see beads of perspiration starting on your forehead. You've just unclenched your right hand and doubled it back into a fist. And now, all of a sudden you have nothing to say."

The man coughed in a wracking, agonized manner, his face twisted with the sharp pain of it.

"Your image is in the mind of every agent we have placed in this country. Someday, somewhere, you will come up against one of us, and it will be a fatal surprise. *You won't know the truth until it's too late for you to do anything but die!*"

With that, he turned and started to climb over the window frame but slipped, falling hard against it, a shard of glass piercing his neck and an obscenity escaping his mouth an instant before he died.

Bartlett reholstered his Colt, turning his attention to the bodies of the man's teenaged sons.

One of the boys was still alive. Bartlett hurried to his side.

"Dad!" the blond-haired, blue-eyed teenager moaned.

"Gone," Bartlett said.

"No!" the boy cried. "And my brother?"

"The same."

A spasm shuddered through the teenager.

"What's your name, son?" Bartlett asked sadly after it had passed.

"Erik, sir . . . we . . . we never hated the Jews the way Dad did. We—"

He started gasping for air.

"Don't talk," Bartlett told him. "I'll get help for you."

"Too late . . . ," the teenager said. "All over . . . it's happening everywhere . . . you think you know what's going on but . . . but you don't."

"We know about *Bloody Winter,* son. And the *Vergeltungswaffen.* We're going to be prepared, Erik. The Nazis can throw at us whatever they want and—"

"*Listen, please!*" Erik begged as he interrupted. "It's much more than just the V-1 or . . . or, even, the V-2 . . . . another . . . kind of missile . . . much smaller . . . lighter . . . and . . . and the U-boats aren't the only sources of launching it."

Bartlett felt ill as he listened, cold sweat covering him.

"The subs will be a diversion of sorts . . . sir," Erik went on, his voice temporarily stronger, the tone even more urgent. "They'll be carrying the V-1s . . . great numbers of them . . . one after the other launched at port cities . . . naval bases. But the second type will be the bigger threat, a whole new version of the V-2s . . . is also going to be launched, sir . . . It will have an extended range large enough to cover many American cities. It . . . it can reach a speed of more than four thousand miles per hour!"

That's 500 miles per hour faster than the V-2, Bartlett thought. *Even at the V-2's range of 225 miles, the devastation would be monstrous. And yet, if he's right, the new version might be capable of striking much deeper into the mainland!*

More than blood was coming up now.

"From Argentina?" Bartlett probed more desperately than he intended. "Is that it, Erik? From secret bases in Argentina?"

The teenager groaned his answer: "*Yes!* But other places, too, islands off the coast of South America, and in the Gulf of Mexico . . . not just . . . just—"

"What targets? How will they be able to hone in on any targets?"

Erik opened his mouth to speak again but no words came this time, his teeth clattering against one another.

Tears started to trickle down his cheeks, and he looked then like nothing more than a frightened little boy, not someone who had participated in an action that was responsible for the deaths of a then-unknown number of FBI agents.

Raising himself slightly he reached out his left hand toward Bartlett, whispering a very faint *"You'll never know . . . what's happening until it's too late . . . we've planted some devices"* before falling back against the floor, his head turned to one side, his body shaken by a sudden, violent spasm as though he had been jolted by the fleeting touch of a live wire. And then he lay still as death descended.

14

Many of the FBI agents were taken to Walter Reed General Hospital. Those who survived did so because they were closer to the windows on that floor. Others had headed for the stairwell. It only took a few who, in their haste and weakened by the gas, tripped and fell, sprawling on top of one another, for the narrow passage to become clogged with their bodies. The deaths in that location were due more to broken ribs piercing vital organs and heads hitting hard steps than the gas itself.

But nearly a dozen did in fact perish directly as a result of being poisoned by the hydrocyanic acid when it was absorbed into their systems through their lungs and the pores in their skin.

Death for these victims was pure agony. The grown men painfully lost control of virtually every normal function of their bodies before they became lifeless, the suffering they had been experiencing evident in the twisted expression on each face.

They look so much like the dead at Dachau, Auschwitz, Mauthausen, Maidenek, or any of the other Nazi camps, Bartlett thought as he surveyed the carnage.

Cut starkly across his mind was something else also compelling, the dying words of a teenage boy.

You'll never know . . . what's happening until it's too late. We've planted some devices . . .

After ambulances and fire trucks and a dozen FBI cars and trucks arrived on the scene, Bartlett got to the agent in charge of the operation, telling him what he had learned from the three saboteurs.

Nodding nervously and frowning, the agent asked, "We've got some good men, but I hear you're the best there is."

The agent hesitated, biting his lower lip for a moment.

"Can you stand some more duty?" he added. "I mean, you *look* as though you could hit the sack now and stay there for a month!"

"That's the way I feel. But I wouldn't sleep much because part of me would still be here anyway."

"So many of us have heard what you've experienced overseas. It's an honor to have you here now with us."

"I hope I can help on *this* side of the Atlantic for a change," Bartlett told him.

"I don't have any doubt about that. My name is Richard Cohen, by the way. I lost some relatives in the camps. If it had been possible, I would have gone over there and kicked some butt right up through the streets of Berlin itself."

"That's coming soon, I think. Hitler now spends a great deal of his time in hiding. He's had a bunker built under the streets of the city. There's some suspicion within the Allied high command that he's prepared to keep on fighting until the last man."

"I wonder if Jews such as myself will ever have the satisfaction of seeing that devil hung or shot through the head? I know it's something we pray for often."

Minutes later, the team of FBI explosives experts, including Jack Hibbert, wearing gas masks fitted over special airtight suits, was sent into the building to conduct a thorough search for bombs and whatever else seemed suspicious.

Stephen Bartlett decided to stay with them for as long as his seriously depleted energies managed to hold out, figuring he owed that to the men who had died, especially if he could find clues that perhaps the others might miss.

Poor Natalie and Andrew, he thought, wondering wistfully what it would be like someday to have a normal life with his wife and son, a life not subject to calls in the early morning about one catastrophe or the other. *There has been so much of that over the years, even before war itself broke out.*

Recollections surfaced of some early explosives consulting work he had done in the United States before being sent to Europe. The work had put him on the periphery of antiunion violence as well as the occasional mob wars that broke out between the various mafioso families during the closing years of Al Capone's reign. That was before Lucky Luciano was able to orchestrate a period of relative peace on the organized crime scene nationwide, his methods in accomplishing this brutal but effective for fifteen long years.

I wonder what will happen if any of their business interests are endangered by the activities of this network of undercover agents, Bartlett mused, *if a mafioso son or daughter is killed in an explosion or fatally poisoned by contaminated water.*

One part of him relished the payback factor as far as the Nazis were concerned; the other saw all too clearly the probability that innocent people would be drawn into the crossfire between the two groups.

The agents searching the OSS headquarters building found no bombs or timing devices even though several of their detection units were being triggered.

"I don't understand it," Bartlett mused out loud, as an adrenaline rush did its sudden work in clearing his weary mind, if only for awhile. "That guy and his kids were *finished* with their work. They were about to leave the building when we surprised them. They *must* have accomplished their mission! Your instruments agree. They wouldn't be sounding like berserk alarm clocks if that weren't the case!"

"But we've searched everywhere," commented Jack Hibbert, who had insisted upon joining them. "*Nothing!* What were they doing here?"

"They weren't sent after any files apparently. There was nothing on any of them, no papers, no exposed film!"

The alarms on their devices continued loudly but not on all three floors. As soon as the agents moved away from the second and made it to the third, nothing seemed to trigger them and the alarms stopped.

"A collective malfunction of our equipment?" Hibbert speculated. "It could be, of course, but nothing like that's happened before. Besides, these things are checked so completely day in and day out that, well, one failure might occur but *not* on every last one of the devices. Hoover would have a fit, and I mean a *big* one, if that were ever allowed to happen."

Finally, the air inside the building tested clear of poisonous fumes, and to the relief of everyone, they were able to shed their awkward and limiting protective clothing.

Bartlett returned to the third floor just as the bodies of the two teenagers and their father were being carried out on stretchers.

"The father looked a little bizarre perhaps," he observed, "like a parody of a mad commandant at one of the extermination camps.

But the boys . . . they seemed like older editions of my own son, Andrew!"

He asked the medics pushing the gurneys to stop while he studied the three bodies.

He noticed one detail that had been missed earlier.

Flecks of a silvery substance on their fingertips.

"Wait," he said, "I see something. It looks a little like silver-colored paint," he surmised, "the kind found on cheap watch-bands."

Hibbert also glanced at their fingers after Bartlett had finished.

"That seems like all it really is," he agreed matter-of-factly. "Or am I missing something, Stephen?"

"Was it there when they arrived, which means we may never know what significance it has, if any? Or did these three get it on their fingers *as a result of* whatever they were doing here?"

"Nothing was found that suggested anything being painted over, Stephen," Hibbert told him. "We missed those flecks because of the helmets on the airtight suits, which, as you know, distort vision slightly. Those flecks were far too small to be seen then, but that wouldn't have been the case with fresh paint on a wall or elsewhere, especially that color. It reminds me of chromium. Anything like that would not have slipped by unnoticed."

Bartlett tried to be nonchalant.

"Then it's probably nothing," he spoke.

"But you're not convinced of that, are you?"

"I'm never convinced when I find myself unable to explain something," Bartlett acknowledged.

He saw an envelope on top of one of the desks.

"I'm going to scrape off whatever I can for the lab analysts."

"I'll help," Hibbert volunteered.

"Thanks."

Bartlett sighed with great weariness after they had finished gathering flakes of the silvery material.

"It's been a very *long* day," he said, a headache pounding at his temples, and weakness setting in from lack of sleep and food.

"And it ends in a short while," a voice spoke in back of them.

Hibbert froze as he heard it, but Bartlett had learned not to be surprised by the sudden intrusions of J. Edgar Hoover.

"Agent Hibbert, take care of everything," the FBI director said. "I'm going to see to it that Bartlett here gets some rest."

After telling his driver to take the rest of the night off, once again, out of earshot, Hoover offered to drive Bartlett to his home, and once again he accepted.

The two men sat in silence for the first few minutes of the drive.

Bartlett's insides were trembling from the stress of the past several hours as he looked at the nearly empty streets, some with darkened homes lining them, a few with office buildings or stores on either side.

How unaware they are, he thought. *Most of these people realize only what is going on so close to where they live or work. They have no idea whether a friend or a relative or a stranger they happen to see is working willingly or otherwise to destroy the United States from within. Hitler has been successful in sending perhaps more than a hundred undercover agents into this country. If he can't defeat us on the battlefield, he's going to try to do so right in our backyards, strewing the land with the bodies of innocent men, women, and children!*

Finally, Hoover spoke.

"Casey thought only I should tell you something else," he said, as they were pulling out of "official" Washington, with its various governmental and other agencies, and heading toward the suburbs. "These moments you and I have here offer the best opportunity. He said that you would find him free at any time if you needed to talk afterward."

Bartlett felt a chill push through his exhaustion, grab him at the base of his skull, and work its way down his spine.

"What is it, sir?" he asked.

"Something more than a simple meeting with a mafioso don is going on," Hoover told him, "something far more involved."

He was looking straight ahead, not taking his eyes off the road nor relaxing his grip on the steering wheel.

"We had already been in touch with Benedetto Vincenzo Santapaola before he and you came in contact with one another," he continued. "Once again he seemed ready to slam the door in our faces, as always. But now, your encounter with Santapaola has allowed us the link we needed."

Bartlett failed to understand what Hoover was getting to at first.

"You probably don't know what I'm talking about, Stephen. That's understandable. May I speak with utter candor?"

"Certainly," Bartlett assured him.

Hoover cleared his throat.

"If anything goes wrong with this," he spoke with almost exaggerated slowness, "we'll need a scapegoat."

Bartlett said nothing.

"In the event the press gets hold of what we'll be starting with Santapaola, it could be very embarrassing for the bureau and for the OSS."

"And so I would be blamed in that eventuality, sir?"

Hoover's hands nervously moved up and down on the steering wheel.

"Santapaola conducts himself by gut feelings more than anything else, it seems. And his gut feeling is that *you* are the only government man with whom he wants any such contact. No one else is acceptable."

"I hear that you are a decent man," Santapaola spoke with apparent admiration. "We could help you regarding Bloody Winter, you know."

"But I'm not the one who decides—," Bartlett protested.

"We could help you," Santapaola repeated, "but no one else."

"Why me?"

"You once put your own life on the line for some friends of mine . . . partisans in Europe. Now I have to do the same as a point of honor. Or does it surprise you that someone such as myself knows the meaning of the word?"

"Why hasn't he tried to contact me if he felt that way?"

"He knew that there was no way any of his men would be allowed anywhere near you. There had to be a right moment. It's not something that can be predicted. It just happens."

Bartlett nodded, his shoulders slumping.

Hoover noticed this and spoke up, "I wonder, Stephen, if being in the midst of Nazi Germany somehow seemed any more unsafe than you feel right now."

"You have a point, sir," he admitted.

"Casey and I would understand if you turned this assignment down," Hoover assured him.

"And then the longshoremen go on strike for who knows how long. After a very short time, the war effort feels the impact. Forgive me for putting it like this, sir, but how can I turn it down while knowing *that?*"

Hoover smiled warmly as he replied, "You are remarkable, Stephen. I admire you a great deal, more than I can ever say. I know that Casey feels as I do."

Bartlett's house was just ahead. Hoover stopped the car in front, and got out. The two men walked up to the front porch and stood there for a moment.

The FBI director extended his left hand.

As Bartlett shook it, he noticed that Hoover was trembling slightly.

"Sir, are you all right?" he asked.

"If power makes me all right, as you say, then I am all right, because, yes, I do have that power."

Bartlett wanted to talk in more detail, but he knew that his exhaustion would not make him very articulate.

"Sir?" he asked. "What would you say about meeting in a day or two to talk . . . with no one else around?"

"I *would* like that, Stephen, I would like that very much."

He turned to go back to his car.

Wearing a powder-blue robe with white lace around the edges, Natalie Bartlett opened the front door, and blushed as she saw Hoover.

"How are you, sir?" she asked, trying to appear unruffled.

"I am perfectly fine, Mrs. Bartlett," he replied.

Just then, Andrew, looking *very* sleepy, came around from behind his mother and stood just outside the doorway.

His face paled when he saw who was with his father.

Hoover looked at the attractive, sandy-haired woman and the nine-year-old boy and then at Stephen Bartlett. "You are a very fortunate man, you know. With such a family to return to and with that rock-solid faith of yours, you seem to lack for nothing in your life, Stephen. Do not ever lose sight of what you have here. Keep that in the forefront of your mind day after day."

He smiled with a curious wistfulness.

"Not everyone is as blessed as you are," he added, almost in a whisper, before walking back to his car, getting in, and riding off through a slight mist tinged with an early-November chill.

15

When he was in the United States, Andrew Bartlett went to a private grade school located in the suburbs, which was also attended by numerous sons and daughters of several influential Washington, D.C., politicians, diplomats, attorneys, and other members of the power elite of those days.

His parents had debated about the wisdom of subjecting him to a peer group of that sort, given, as it undoubtedly was, to a certain level of arrogance inherited from the influential parents. But they had decided that the security measures in place during those war-time years were of overriding importance, not to mention the school's acknowledged scholastic excellence.

Stephen Bartlett had to leave that evening and fly to New Jersey for a meeting with Benedetto Vincenzo Santapaola. He would have preferred to stay home and rest that day, but Andrew was participating in a soccer game at the school, and as a father, he knew he could not avoid going even if he fell asleep in the bleachers.

Half an hour after the game started, he excused himself and walked back to the adjacent school building.

He noticed a crew of maintenance employees mopping the floor and scrubbing the walls as well as hauling in fresh pipes, along with paint cans and brushes—considerable activity for a Saturday.

He went up to one of them and introduced himself.

"You've got a great school here," he said pleasantly as he extended his hand.

"That's what they say," the other man muttered as he shook hands rather limply for someone of his not inconsiderable size.

"Say, where's a restroom?" Bartlett asked.

"Down the hallway and to your left," the man replied amiably, a paintbrush in his other hand.

Bartlett thanked him and walked in that direction, glancing at photos and drawings on the corridor walls, some of the latter by very young children expressing their hope and their innocence.

After a minute or two he saw the door marked BOYS.

As he pushed it open and went inside, he thought he heard the sound of a radio nearby, an announcer perhaps, talking fast but his voice partially muffled by static.

After he had used the toilet and was about to wash his hands, he realized that the radio had ceased.

He turned the hot water knob.

Nothing.

He tried it again.

Still nothing.

"No wonder they've got a whole crew here!" he remarked out loud. "They'll need to get everything fixed by Monday."

Regretting that he couldn't wash his hands, he left the bathroom and was walking back down the same corridor when he noticed something else.

Gone.

The half-dozen men he had seen earlier were now nowhere around. Their buckets and paint cans also were gone.

Paint cans!

Bartlett could never feel certain that he had a kind of sixth sense about such things, and he harbored serious reservations about any individuals who claimed special "powers" of one sort or another.

But the truth was that the nerves on the back of his neck were tingling.

Where are they? Bartlett thought, looking at the half-painted walls. *And that sound—an announcer giving a weather report or a—?*

Shaking his head, he knew that he was being foolish, overreacting to some quite innocent circumstances.

Lunch break, he told himself. *It's as simple as that!*

As he approached the back door, he noticed silver specks on the edge of his thumb!

Suddenly his throat went very dry.

He reached instinctively for his pistol, but he hadn't brought it with him to the soccer game.

Once again, he felt stupid.

They don't pay me for being skittish! he scolded himself.

Just then, the janitor he'd met minutes before came out into the hallway from one of the schoolrooms.

"Did you find the restroom, sir?" he asked pleasantly.

"I did. Thanks."

As the man was walking away, Bartlett called after him, "I got some silvery stuff on my hand, I think, when I shook yours. What in the world is it?"

"Oh, yes, we're replacing some of the pipes in the plumbing system here, recoating the rest. That's just the paint we've been using. You probably tried to wash your hands but there was no water, right?"

Bartlett nodded.

"Everything's been turned off. No big deal, though. It'll all be functioning just fine by Monday."

Bartlett thanked him and was opening the door to go outside when he noticed that the man's voice had changed very slightly, and there was, for an instant, the faintest trace of a German accent to it.

Spinning around on one heel, Bartlett asked, "Where are you from?"

"A small town in the Midwest. Why?" the other man responded.

"I thought I detected an accent."

"You probably did. German, wasn't it?"

"That's right."

"Frankly I try to fight it but it slips through now and then."

"Why do you bother?" Bartlett asked, as he studied the man.

"You see, my folks—my parents, brothers and sisters, and I—settled in the United States a very long time ago. We arrived here after leaving Dusseldorf. None of us was ashamed of our heritage until the war started.

"I never did have much of an accent—Mom and Dad had enough for all of us, I guess—but these days, I try to get whatever is left of it out of my voice. What the Nazis are doing back home makes me want to flush everything in my life that is German down one of the sewer pipes in this school! Can you understand what I'm saying, mister?"

Bartlett smiled awkwardly, apologized for being so inquisitive, and went outside.

The game was over in an hour. Andrew's team won.

They celebrated by having hamburgers, french fries, and milkshakes, then they strolled together through a park along the Potomac, watching the city's lights come on as the sun went down. Finally they headed home, grateful for those few hours together.

A message had been slipped under the front door.

The longshoremen's strike was called off. Santapaola had decided to act without seeing Bartlett first.

"But why did he do this?" Bartlett asked Casey after calling the OSS director at home. "What made him change his mind?"

"*Bloody Winter,* Stephen. Santapaola knows about it too."

"How could he?"

Hesitation.

"You understand, don't you, that he has links with that Hyannis Port crowd?"

"I suspected as much. But they've never been my favorite people. I don't know much more than that."

"When Joe Kennedy's National Socialists connections became known, Santapaola went crazy. He wanted to attack the whole family, leaving only the women and children alive. He'd come to think that their conduct constituted a flagrant act of treason. But he was canny enough not to let them suspect how he felt. They're still allowing him into their inner sanctum. And all Santapaola is doing is waiting for the right moment. At least this is what we are surmising. There are *some* things about which the guy hasn't been exactly forthcoming."

Bartlett thought for a moment then said, "So Santapaola found out about *Bloody Winter* through some of their German sources during one of the times he spent at Hyannis Port? I'm coming right over. No time can be wasted."

"Stephen, Stephen, listen to me. Get some rest. I'll have a car pick you up at eight in the morning. You're no good to me, to your country, if you have no energy left. Your thinking's going to be fuzzy at best. I need you in top form. Listen to me now, OK?"

Bartlett thanked him and hung up, sitting beside the phone for a moment.

Natalie found him there in the downstairs hallway a few moments later.

"It's late," she spoke. "Are you coming to bed?"

He looked at her, smiled.

"I love you very much," he said.

"What's this all about?" she asked, blushing because he had said it with such passion.

"I'm just realizing that no matter what happens around us, you're always here. I don't know what I'd do without you."

16

By the time they had crawled into bed, it was nearly midnight. Exhausted, they chose not to make love but just to rest in one another's arms until sleep came.

Five hours later, the phone rang.

Bartlett groped for the phone on a small, round night table beside the bed, his fingers closing numbly around it and lifting it to his ear before he was entirely aware of what he was doing.

"Yes?" he half-groaned.

"Casey here," the OSS director told him urgently. "You must listen very carefully, Stephen."

Bartlett's pulse quickened.

"Go ahead," he mumbled.

"Get yourself and your family dressed as quickly as possible."

"What's going on, sir?"

Natalie was awakening.

"Stephen, what is it?" she asked.

He put a finger on his lips as he listened to Casey's voice on the phone, the expression on his face tense. She didn't persist.

"You *must* leave your house as quickly as humanly possible."

Bartlett could think of only one reason.

"A bomb?"

"Perhaps."

"How did you find out?"

"It seems you really did hit it off with Hoover. He feels very protective now toward you, Natalie, and Andrew. He wants to make sure you all are safe. So he sent two agents by your house to make sure everything is all right."

"What made him suspect something could be wrong?"

"Hoover chalked it up to some sort of premonition. You might have another description. Whatever the case, the agents were on their way back to FBI headquarters from that building you'd left yesterday."

Bartlett knew that Casey wasn't a man given to melodrama, so his manner now seemed all the more terrifying.

"They picked up that same strange reaction on their instruments, but this time it was coming from your house, Stephen. They contacted Hoover immediately, and he ordered two more cars of agents to join them."

A pause, as Casey sucked in his breath.

"Whatever was planted and couldn't be uncovered is now also somewhere in your house. *Please hurry!*"

Bartlett thanked Casey and hung up the receiver.

"You're so tense," Natalie observed as she wrapped her arms around his chest and rested her chin on his back. "What was that all about?"

He told her what Casey had said.

"We've been here most of the time, except for the soccer game yesterday," she said. "No one could have gotten in and left without either of us knowing about it if we were here!"

"We can't take a chance. There's no telling *when* it was planted inside, whatever it is. They can accomplish what they have to and get out quietly and cleanly. Their whole lives have become bound up in this war, whether it's in Europe or right here in Washington. They know they can't afford to be sloppy."

Natalie hugged herself, looking around at the familiar surroundings: the floral-print wall-paper, the dark-mahogany dresser, the makeup table with its round mirror ringed by miniature light bulbs.

"To think that . . . that those devils invaded this . . . . this . . . ," she replied, her voice shrill, some panic in it.

He kissed her with considerable passion.

"If we move quickly and the men being sent here do their job, we just might have it to return to, my love," he whispered. "Think of that and nothing else right now."

She looked at him with great love and admiration.

"Let's go," she said simply.

After jumping out of bed, Bartlett grabbed a fresh shirt and slacks, and Natalie pulled on a sweater and some jeans.

"It's cold this time of year," he reminded her.

She threw over to him the same coat he'd worn the night before, and she chose a heavy jacket for herself.

Andrew was already awake, stirred by the noise they were making.

"What's going on?" he asked as he stood in the doorway of their bedroom.

"Get dressed now, Andrew," Natalie told the nine-year-old. "We're going outside as quickly as we can."

The boy's eyes widened.

"Trouble?" he asked.

"Trouble," his father confirmed.

Andrew dashed back to his room.

I was convinced we would be free of this, Bartlett thought as he and Natalie stood in the hallway outside their son's room. *Instead, so soon after we come back from Europe, something else is entering our lives, threatening us.*

He squeezed her hand a little tighter, glad to have this woman by his side.

As soon as they had reached the front door and were headed outside, two black sedans were pulling up at the curb, joining another that was already there.

Half a dozen men jumped out.

"Bomb squad," Bartlett assured his wife and son.

"A bomb? Here?" Andrew blurted out. "I've got to go back and get a few things from my room. Please, Dad! I gotta!"

"Too late, son. Not enough time."

They stepped aside, and the men, nodding at them, hurried into the house.

"I'm proud of you," Natalie said, smiling.

"For doing what?" Bartlett asked, surprised.

"For restraining yourself and not going in with them."

"How did you know I was fighting the urge?" he joked.

"I know by the way you blink," she told him. "When you're struggling with something, you blink a lot faster, as though there's a speck in your eyes and you're trying to get it out before it irritates or scratches the cornea."

He laughed, and the three of them hugged one another as they waited.

One of the agents coming from the house spread his hands out, palms upward, a frown on his face.

"Believe it or not, we couldn't find anything," he announced. "This is the second time that's happened. Strangest thing!"

Another man next to him saw that he had forgotten to turn off the black, square detection device strapped to his waist.

He was about to do just that when he realized that the needle in the half-moon-shaped indicator window was beginning to register something.

"Impossible!" he said. "They should keep this equipment in better condition. Being sloppy can prove *real* dangerous."

He looked sheepishly at Stephen Bartlett and said, "What about your guys? Are they sharper than this?"

"I hope so. I trained them."

The man was turning away when he stood still abruptly.

"It's stopping now," he commented. "It's—"

He turned back toward Bartlett again.

"But when I aim it in your direction, it goes crazy!" he exclaimed. "What in the devil is wrong with this thing?"

Bartlett thought only of one thing then.

A narrow, white envelope filled with silvery particles stuck absentmindedly into the interior pocket of the coat he was wearing!

Bartlett took it out and held it directly in front of the detection device, which worked somewhat along the lines of a customary Geiger-Müller counter but was much more sophisticated, according to the standards of that day.

The needle on top seemed to be having some kind of electrical spasm.

"This is a new device since I was in the States last," Bartlett commented. "Tell me: Is it capable only of detecting *explosive* devices? Under normal circumstances, can anything *else* be picked up by it?"

"Very astute," the agent congratulated him. "It *is*, in a way, a kind of de facto dual-purpose instrument. This ingenious little box is able to pick up anything capable of *receiving* shortwave transmissions because, in effect, it sends out its own kind of radiolike signal and alerts us to when it has *connected*, for want of a better word. Frankly ham radio operators hate it."

"It must play havoc with their sets!"

"That it does, and any other kind of radio reception in the area. We can *count* on complaints by the truckload whenever we have to use these devices in any great quantity."

"What about air traffic? Isn't it dangerous to the navigational instruments in planes?"

"It is every bit that. That's why we are required to check with the airports before we use these in any concentrated number, though a single unit isn't really so much of a danger. Otherwise, it's not inconceivable that we could succeed in saving a building from being blown up by detecting any bombs that had been planted inside but, if not careful, cause more than one plane to crash. It's not a good trade-off!"

"So you had a window of opportunity a short while ago, and you used it?" Bartlett suggested.

"That's right. But only in quick spurts. Turn it on, aim it, then turn it off. That's just about what we had to do. We certainly found out there were no bombs inside, so it excelled for us in that particular mission inside your house, but now look at *this* bizarre reaction."

Bartlett handed the envelope to him.

"Tear open one corner," he requested, "and look inside."

The agent did this.

"Paint?" he asked. "Ordinary paint, is that what you're showing me?"

"Ordinary paint wouldn't drive that device of yours crazy," Bartlett stressed. "I think it could be something far more important than what we see in those few specks. Will you get it to your lab guys right away?"

"That I'll do," the agent assured.

"Any idea how long testing will take?"

"We should have something to report by noon or so."

"Don't bother to call me," Bartlett told him. "I'll be there. And I think director Casey will probably want to join us."

"Because of *this*?" the agent asked, notably unconvinced that they were on the verge of discovering anything important.

"I hate to say it but I have a feeling about the stuff," Bartlett said, " . . . a *terrible* feeling."

17

They hadn't seen anything like it.

On the rectangular-shaped, pockmarked old table before them was something that, judging from its appearance, could have been a tiny piece of transparent celluloid, but which was considerably more flexible and quite a bit thinner, so much so that it was difficult for them to see when it was held with tweezers.

"Where did you find that?" Casey asked.

"Embedded in the paint," the short, pudgy lab technician explained succinctly.

"You mean it had become stuck to the paint?" Bartlett added.

"Not *on* the paint, although I understand how you could have assumed that. When I said *in* the paint, I wasn't using a figure of speech, I'm afraid. But more about that in a moment."

Casey scratched the back of his head, as puzzled as Bartlett was.

"Now I'm going to put it under the microscope," the technician explained. "You will be *amazed!*"

He slipped the filmlike substance onto a slide, which he then placed beneath the lens of a bulky but powerful microscope.

"See for yourself, gentlemen," he said.

Casey looked first, then Bartlett.

What they saw was something that had been miniaturized to such a degree that it seemed no bigger than a colony of amoebas . . . a network of the tiniest imaginable wires connected to a series of semi-oval shapes.

"Seen enough?" the technician asked.

"Yes . . . ," Casey replied warily. "But what *have* we seen, anyway? It looks like a photograph of something."

"I'll admit that that was precisely my impression initially. But I looked at it from different angles, various magnifications. It isn't flat.

It has depth. And so I came to the conclusion that it's not a photograph *of* an object but an object in and of itself or, more appropriately, a series of objects."

He grinned mischievously.

"But the wonders don't stop there," the technician went on. "I isolated what you just saw from one of those flecks of paint. There were others like it in other flecks, absorbed *into* the paint apparently much more completely than, say, confetti sprinkled over wet cement."

"But what's the purpose?" Casey probed. "What does it *do?*"

"That is both the miracle as well as the nightmare," the technician replied. "Have you heard of John Bardeen, Walter H. Brattain, and William Shockley?"

"Of course," the OSS director replied. "They're supposed to be working on a secret project to invent what they're calling a transistor. The full name is point-contactor transistor, I believe. What's the connection?"

"What you have seen *is* a transistor!"

"You can't be serious!" scoffed Casey.

"I am, I assure you. Each of these little specks of silver paint contains at least one transistor of sorts, though it is primitive in some respects. From what I hear about Bardeen, Brattain, and Shockley, theirs will be much more advanced and will be capable of a number of uses. By contrast, what we have here has been created with just one *raison d'être*. Therein lies the mad genius of its design, epitomized by its size."

"Go on . . . ," Casey prodded, losing patience with the technician's plodding, somewhat teasing manner. "What is its reason for being?"

"To act as a simple but effective mini-receiver for shortwave transmissions," he said, smiling sardonically because he knew how they would react.

Neither man disappointed him.

They stood next to one another in the gray-toned old laboratory, where the bullet that had killed Abraham Lincoln had been sent to be analyzed some eighty years earlier, located in a building that was nearly a century old. Their faces had gone pale with shock, their minds racing ahead to the implications so starkly evident in what they were being told.

A man with a paintbrush could wield more power than somebody else with a machine gun! thought Bartlett, the images his imagination conjured up more terrifying than any found in a fanciful Hollywood horror film of that era.

Casey found it necessary to grab a nearby chair and sit down.

"It's quite straightforward actually," the technician continued, with some admiration. "I imagine it was an outgrowth of their ingenious microdot process, which enables the Nazis to reduce a photograph of a large sheet of paper, even a very big map, first to the size of a postage stamp and from there, on down to that of an ordinary period at the end of a sentence.

"I can picture two groups of Nazi mad scientist-inventors getting together, one bragging about the *Mikropunkt* they had come up with and the other trumpeting a much more enlarged version of the same transistor you saw. How Hitler and the other thugs must have jumped for joy when the two groups united their disparate inventions to come up with *that!*"

He pointed to the microscope for emphasis.

"So here is what happens: These little devils are miniaturized and then submerged within a canister of ordinary paint rather than pressed to the surface of a sheet of paper, as with the *Mikropunkt*. Certainly *that* technology is extraordinary but it becomes banal in comparison to what we're looking at here.

"When that paint is subsequently spread on, say, pipes or electrical wiring and dries, it seems innocent enough, indistinguishable from ordinary paint of that color and texture, which tends to be thicker and more durable since it is often used outdoors on water towers, chain-link fences, exposed plumbing, and the like."

What he was mentioning included some of the more mundane images throughout the United States, their commonplaceness now chilling in view of what they could represent.

"Look at what that means, gentlemen," he added. "You must agree that the consequences could be terrifying!"

The technician was holding a flimsy wooden model of an airplane above the silver specks, which he had spread out single file on the lab table in front of him. He swooped it down in a sudden arc toward these, then collapsed the model into a crumbled ball between his fingers and threw it in a nearby bucket.

"I thought that little demonstration would crystallize my point as graphically as possible," he told Casey and Bartlett. "Now the enemy can actually send in his rockets, with these infernal little devices guiding each one to a target like well-trained homing pigeons.

But that model plane I just trashed also serves as an example of quite another phenomenon they are capable of precipitating."

He had been looking down at the flecks, gently touching several with one of his fingers. Now his head shot up straight and his gaze locked in on Casey's and Bartlett's own with such unexpected intensity that they felt more than a little unnerved.

"Taken as a whole, each transistor is unquestionably capable of the fearsome potential to play utter havoc with the navigational systems of any of our domestic planes, military or commercial, that are unfortunate enough to come within their range. That range, by the way, is multiplied in direct correlation to how many of them happen to be grouped together, i.e., the whole being far greater than the sum of its parts."

Casey spoke in reaction to that potential series of catastrophes but mechanically, his voice drained of feeling, his body numb.

"How many of our bases have been compromised? How many of our electrical plants? Our factories? Our—"

"The Nazis don't need bombs now," Bartlett exclaimed, "just a few cans of paint and some brushes!"

"Finding out who the saboteurs are as well as where they've struck already *and* where they are *going* to hit next is an impossible task," commented Casey nervously. "Our enemy has the crucial advantage of weeks or months of planning."

The lab technician had been wearing a pair of wire-rimmed glasses, and now he took them off and twirled them around absentmindedly between his fingers.

"In a single three-foot-by-three-inch section of this *fortified* paint, which is what it is, of course, spread carefully over just one piece of nearly inaccessible pipe at any airport, any factory where grenades or bullets or bombs are manufactured, any assembly plant for tanks or jeeps or other vehicles, well, you get the idea," he told them straightforwardly. "Why, there could be dozens of the little buggers even on the narrow little arms of these glasses. That's what we're going to have to be dealing with, and I don't know how we even start!"

He slid the glasses toward their end of the table.

"Isn't that extraordinary, though? Hitler's scientists have come up with an invention possessing the capability of endangering air traffic over all this country at the same time they're guiding toward some well-chosen targets whatever secret new rocket the German military decides to throw at us."

CODE NAME: BLOODY WINTER

As Stephen Bartlett was driving home, he realized how fortunate it was that he didn't have an accident because his attention was more on what he had just learned than on traffic conditions.

If the Nazis had been able to develop a transistor so small and paper-thin that many of them could be embedded into a small section of paint and remain undetected, there wasn't any way such a striking master plan could be stopped before so many of the devices had been planted that uncovering them would be wholly unfeasible.

I don't envision anyone at the German high command getting a twinge of conscience and drawing us a map of the targets being compromised, he thought.

Since it was Sunday, Bartlett expected to see no substantial numbers of painters working and, in fact, there were none. But plumbers were another story, and he noticed trucks parked in front of three houses several miles apart on his route home. Plumbing emergencies had brought them out, even on a weekend.

As he drove past each, he had to fight an urge to stop and confront whoever was involved and search their truck for some silver paint.

They're not going to go after simple residences, he told himself. They want government buildings, factories, and airports.

Bartlett turned off the main highway toward the suburb where he and his family lived. On his right was a gated mini-community of homes whose residents worked in important jobs at the state or war departments and other agencies together with some Congressmen who had made considerable amounts of money in the business world before they became senators or members of the House of Representatives.

Even when they're away from the Capitol, he thought, *they seem to have to seek one another's company! How many deals are made on tennis courts and in family dining rooms where nobody has any control over men who are supposed to be serving the people instead of their own, often extravagant interests?*

The streets were being torn up, detracting from the carefully calculated beauty and neatness of the neighborhood.

Sewer pipes were being installed.

Everything up to date, at taxpayers' expense, Bartlett mused cynically as he drove on past, catching out of the corner of his eye several men who were touching up portions of the pipes with fresh paint.

Stupid! he mused. *They'll never be seen. They don't have to look brand-new and all freshly painted when they're—*

Fresh *silver-colored* paint.

He slammed his foot down on the brake, holding the steering wheel for a moment as he tried to calm his nerves, tried to think over the situation, tried to see how idiotic it was of him to give a sinister turn to something so simple.

How many new sewer pipes during the past few weeks had been placed under the streets of American towns and cities? How many plumbers were not that at all but instead cleverly infiltrated German spies?

He burst out laughing.

And then he stopped, abruptly, when he heard the erratic sound of an airplane in obvious trouble. He got out of the car and looked up at the sky, squinting against the glare of the overhead sun.

A passenger plane.

It seemed to be descending, then it pulled up and regained some altitude, only to start to drop again, this time at a faster rate.

Andrew's school is located in that direction! he recalled. *But this is Sunday, so there'll be nobody inside, no—*

Bartlett got back into his car and continued driving toward home. Less than two blocks away from it, he again saw the plane to his left, spiraling completely out of control and heading, it seemed, directly toward the school.

Thank God, Andrew's not there! he told himself. *Thank God no one else is today. Otherwise, hundreds of kids could be involved.*

Bartlett pulled up in front of the wood-frame bungalow in which he and his family had lived for a number of years when they weren't overseas. He jumped out, racing up the walkway.

Whether the school was empty or not, any action against it represented a clear escalation of the espionage dimension of the war that was certain to generate public panic if the news were to leak out before the various federal authorities got their act together and either squelched it somehow or prepared a reasonable-sounding explanation intended to defuse the situation.

Natalie was already opening the door as he made it to the front porch.

"That plane!" she said, her eyes wide, a look of panic on her face. "I saw it just as you arrived. It's heading toward the school, I think."

"I know, I know!" he interrupted. "I've got to make some calls. Get some help just in case. Tell Andrew to stay here and —"

"Oh, Stephen, I can't!" she exclaimed. "He's not here!"

He froze at those words.

"Where is our son?" Bartlett asked, though some sick feeling inside him provided the answer before she could utter the words. "Where is he, Natalie?"

"Andrew's at school!" she said, her voice high-pitched. "There's a special picnic going on in the playground."

Natalie was starting to shake from head to foot, her mind racing ahead to what might be happening in only a few moments, her hand going to her mouth as she tried to stifle a sudden, loud cry.

Bartlett put his arms around his wife and she rested her head briefly on his shoulder.

"Andrew helped his Sunday school class organize it for some underprivileged kids from the inner city," she managed to say. "*He's there right now, Stephen!*"

18

The school was only a few miles away from his home.

As he drove in that direction, ignoring stop signs and traffic lights, Bartlett saw people of all ages hurrying from their homes, alarmed at the erratic sound of the plane passing so close overhead, which broke the quiet of that calm Sunday afternoon. Most were pointing as well as talking, men in sports shirts and old, baggy pants, some with pipes or cigars or cigarettes, women in casual housedresses or fancy robes, several sporting old-fashioned curlers in their hair.

Others seemed, or pretended to seem, not much concerned at all, showing only mild curiosity for the moment, because, Bartlett supposed, they pooh-poohed the possibility that any of *them* would be involved in some kind of catastrophe.

But it could crash anywhere, Bartlett thought. *Scores of you could die in another Nazi-inspired inferno, yet so many of you treat it almost as a joke, the same way even some of the Jews did early in Hitler's rise to power in Germany, convinced that it just couldn't happen in the country of their birth!*

Something about the Germanic temperament occurred to him then, the age-old disregard for mass destruction that was always just below the surface, ready to flare up regardless of how bizarre the justification, and always rooted in hatred—for Jews, for Gypsies, for anyone they viewed as a foreigner.

All of this means nothing to their kind, he told himself, *whether they're disposing of tens of thousands of bodies on battlefields throughout Europe or in the death camps or through sabotage in an American suburban neighborhood. Whatever it takes is fine so long as it enables them to flaunt their supposed racial superiority!*

Seconds before Bartlett reached the school, the plane had precipitously dropped the last few thousand feet, colliding with the flat

147

roof of the brick school building, plowing through it, scattering fragments of glass and wood and tile like bloated bullets, that were nearly as deadly as those fired from guns. It finally shuddered to a halt, the partially collapsed building under its belly, its nose tilted down and burrowed partway into the ground, chunks of asphalt in its path torn up and tossed in every direction, the rear section of the plane pointed at a ninety-degree angle toward the sky.

He slammed on the brakes, the car swerving to his left and ramming into a tree, the steering wheel snapping but not before he was flung to one side, away from it.

For an instant the crash jarred his mind back, to another time: a night in London when the buzz bombs fell and the normalcy of lives from Cadogen Square to Fleet Street and elsewhere was destroyed as old buildings became rubble and human beings were little more than so much blood-soaked debris.

Now, he thought, fully alert once more, *something like that is happening here. This is just the start. How many more planes will crash before the U-boats surface and send the new wave of devastation across the land?*

Screams.

One, then another, then a multitude of them.

Suddenly, Stephen Bartlett could hear a chorus of screams, many of them obviously coming from children.

He opened the door on the passenger's side and rolled out, painfully hitting the street.

Smoke.

And along with it, the odor of leaking oil!

Directly ahead, he could see streams of smoke coming from inside the school.

Getting to his feet, Bartlett steadied himself for a moment, fighting nausea and severe whiplash at the back of his neck. Then, unsteadily, he ran across the street, approaching the silvery chain-link fence that surrounded the playground.

An adult Sunday school teacher with whom he had been acquainted from meetings at the school was stumbling toward him, one hand hanging, paralyzed, by his side, blood dribbling out of his mouth.

"Jordan Maxwell!" Bartlett exclaimed.

The other man tried to speak but was unable to say anything, and then fell straight down, hitting his head hard on the asphalt street. He turned slightly, looking up at Bartlett with an expression of great pain.

CODE NAME: BLOODY WINTER

After taking his pulse and determining that Maxwell was dead, Bartlett stepped back, looked left, then right along the fence and spotted the innocuous little black-and-white signs that proclaimed: CAREFUL! WET PAINT!

It wasn't the guys inside! His mind shouted the unsettling truth. *The one I confronted must have been telling me the truth. Somebody else caused all this destruction and death with only a coat of paint, resurfacing an old rusty fence so that it looked like new!*

Bartlett entered the playground through a gate that had been bent back and ripped off its foundation leaving only jagged poles, their bases still set in concrete.

As he looked for his son, he saw one body after another fall and become, in little more than an instant, blackened, grotesque husks consumed by geysers of flame that shot out of one of the right wing's engines as well as rising up from the basement of the school itself, where the boilers apparently had been damaged sufficiently for them to suddenly ignite.

Children ran to playground exits leading out into the street, or, unthinkingly, back into what was left of the school building, hoping to find some kind of refuge among the ruins. Their clothes torn, several of them blinded by floating red-hot embers or scattered pieces of the propellers and other sections of the plane's crumpled body, the fortunate ones joined friends who took them by the hand and tried to help them as they helped themselves.

Picnic tables were overturned, ears of corn and loaves of bread and fried chicken legs crunched underfoot. The contents of broken bottles of ketchup and pickles and mayonnaise made the asphalt treacherous, and men and children were slipping as they tried to get away from the mushrooming holocaust. Containers of milk broke, and streaks of the slippery white liquid oozed throughout the playground among the children's toys that were broken or torn.

And then there were the scores of men, women, and children on the plane itself, those still alive fighting to open escape doors that had become blocked by debris on the outside or bent in such a way as to be inoperable. The captain had remained in the cockpit, unable to get out before he died, wedged partway through what was now an open window frame devoid of glass.

Bartlett jumped onto one wing that had been twisted nearly in half by the impact.

There was no way to open the doors from the outside except with a specific octagonal-shaped key that only an authorized airport attendant would have had. Any override provided as a safety measure to be used in an emergency situation had apparently been rendered useless by the complete failure of the plane's electrical system.

Without the key, Bartlett could do nothing but direct the passengers toward the cockpit. The windshield there ran from one side of the plane around to the other, and the glass had been shattered when the plane crashed. At least some of the thinner passengers could get out by scrambling through the opening, but that was not a very high percentage of those inside.

He saw a number of them shove past others and head in that direction.

None made it.

The plane was seized by a massive, rumbling sound so loud, so violent that the explosion that immediately followed seemed an anticlimax. Suddenly the tail section crashed downward from its bent-up position.

Bartlett was wrenched off the wing, landing on his back on the asphalt, every organ in his body seemingly jarred. He stumbled away from the plane, the expressions on the faces of the people looking down at him through the portal windows accusing him of doing nothing but standing by and watching them die, which was, of course, exactly what happened.

As it turned out, the main cabin of the plane was largely intact. There were cracks in the fuselage but just one was large enough to let any of the passengers crawl through; it was close to the rear where the tail had partway dropped down, putting a strain on the metal next to it, a strain that quickly sliced open the cabin at that point. But the crack was narrow at best and edged with jagged pieces, some every bit as sharp as well-honed knives.

And yet it seemed the only way to safety for anyone inside since the explosion had virtually flattened the cockpit, blocking the only other escape route that made any sense, at least for some of the passengers.

One after the other, they scrambled toward it.

Two of the smaller women got through, their clothes badly torn, cuts, and gashes over their midsections.

But after them, no others made it out.

A large man followed them but became stuck in that narrow opening, his body squirming for a few seconds before it drooped lifelessly.

Bartlett turned away as he saw other passengers reach out and tear at the man's body, several of them making what sounded like animalistic snarling sounds, pulling him away. Having succeeded, however grotesquely, they then attempted to squeeze through the same limited opening only to become stuck themselves, irretrievably blocking the tenuous exit as their bodies piled up.

"Andrew! My son, my son! Where are you?" screamed Bartlett, his voice hopelessly muffled by the sounds around him, the crackling of flames, the roar as sections of the school building continued to collapse, the cries of anguished children looking for adults to help them but finding that any who had been at the playground earlier had not survived. Now the terrified youngsters were suddenly left to themselves.

Except for Stephen Bartlett.

They all seemed to spot him at once, some kind of collective sense running through them. One pointed, then another, and in seconds they ran toward him, grabbing at his trouser legs, pulling at his arms, begging him, "Mister, mister, help us! We don't know what to do! Please, please help us!"

Bartlett was forced to admit to himself that he didn't care as much for these children as for his own son, and he was being driven almost to ignore them, since Andrew was not among those who gathered around him.

"I've got to find someone!" he said, desperation choking his voice. "There's the exit. Go for it yourselves. You're not stupid. *Go!*"

A little girl had bumped into him and found his hand; now she was tugging at it.

"I'm blind, mister," she cried. "I'm scared. I don't know what to do."

He looked at the little ones gathered around him, more than a dozen of them. Glancing over their heads, he saw why they needed help even if they were able to get beyond the confines of the playground itself.

The chaos and destruction had started to spread beyond the chain-link fence to the surrounding neighborhood.

Streets joined at an intersection at the north corner of the school were becoming clogged with cars, any number of which had collided with one another. Houses were venting streams of smoke. He saw flames shooting out of what had been picture windows.

The sounds of mob panic filled the air: people running across lawns, their arms loaded with as many belongings as they could manage to carry. They were running into one another, acting quite as desperately as the passengers in the fallen plane.

Projectiles from that vessel had hit some electrical wires above the street, severing them at one end and sending them into the growing throng of panicked men, women, and children, causing the deaths of three who could not get out of the way fast enough and were electrocuted where they stood.

And no help had come as yet from any source.

Where's the bureau? he thought. *Why hasn't Casey done something? There are no fire trucks as yet. Doesn't anybody else know what's happening except the victims?*

"Follow me!" Bartlett shouted.

He picked up the blind girl and made certain the others had joined hands, then he led them through what had become a gauntlet: dangerous pieces of metal on every side, the remains of bodies strewn across their makeshift path, glass from the school's windows underfoot, soft strips of melting rubber nearly liquid to the touch.

"I can't move!" one five-year-old boy cried. "I'm—"

The soles of his shoes had become stuck in a gooey, black, rubbery section on the asphalt on the playground, probably where leaking fuel from the plane had dissolved the asphalt. Another child, a girl, broke away from the line following Stephen Bartlett, helped the boy out of his shoes, lifted him out of the goo, and then walked beside him so he could lean on her, his legs unsteady, one ankle sprained slightly.

As they reached the one gate not blocked, Bartlett hesitated. The scene was almost as nightmarish outside the playground as it was inside.

Get the fire trucks here! Bartlett's mind screamed as raw terror started to wind its tentacles around him, causing cold sweat to soak his clothes, sweat that had nothing to do with the now inferno-like heat. *Those devils in Berlin are sitting back and chortling over all this, hardly able to wait for the time when this will happen again somewhere else in this country!*

And then he saw something that seemed incomprehensible at first.

A small fleet of black limousines and flatbed trucks were pulling up alongside the curb a block down the street to his left, one in back of the other!

"What in the—?" he started to say.

From each vehicle, big men in construction-worker outfits, including hard hats, jumped out and headed up the street for the site.

One of them saw Bartlett and hurried over to him.

"What can we do to help?" he asked brusquely.

"Try to keep the crowd in line."

Bartlett pointed to the out-of-control mass of people a few hundred feet ahead of them at the intersection adjacent to the school.

"Don't let any of them into the playground and especially not in the building. They'll want to look for their children or friends, but it's far too dangerous right now. There's no way of telling if more explosions are going to occur."

Bartlett paused, then asked, "Say, which agency or department sent you? And why the limousines?"

The man laughed.

"Hey, there's no agency . . ."

He paused for effect, then added, "Santapaola sent us!"

"How did he know?" Bartlett reacted, amazed.

The man's eyes narrowed.

"I guess you don't realize that communications are scrambled all over this area. It's a real mess!"

"Then how were *you* tipped off?" Bartlett asked.

"We have our own," the man answered cryptically.

"Is Santapaola here?"

"Yes, he is. He insisted on coming with us . . . wanted to make sure we really did something to help, even if it happened to be dangerous."

He offered to take the blind girl.

Bartlett nodded reluctantly, handing her over to him, amazed at how gently the other man, so rough-looking because of the sheer bulk of his torso and the thick, roughness of his hands, picked her up and carried her back down the street, talking in a kindly manner to soothe the child as much as the circumstances would allow. Then he returned and asked about the other children, and Bartlett agreed that they could be put, for their safety, in the other cars.

Dressed like the other men, Benedetto Vincenzo Santapaola had just gotten out of one of the big cars and was walking up to Bartlett.

"Where is a cop when you need one?" he said, smiling.

"Your man said that communications were chaotic around here."

"That's true. Lots of interference, I guess, because of the wires that have been snapped. But I have several perfectly secure phone lines in one of my houses near here—free, I might add, of FBI wiretaps—and a few at my office. I went ahead and placed an anonymous call to both the FBI and the OSS. Even so, with the good lines, it was tough getting through, but I finally succeeded. I expect they'll be sending help here soon."

"And then you'll leave."

"I've never been comfortable with so many Feds around me. You can hardly blame me for feeling that way. Those guys have been trying to nab me for years."

As Bartlett was about to speak, he heard a familiar voice yelling for him, weak, trembling, a hint of pain in it.

"Andrew!" he called out. "Son, where are you?"

"There he is!" Santapaola said, quickly pointing across the street to a window frame in what remained of the second floor of the school building.

Bartlett looked up, cupping his hands to his mouth, and shouted, "Andrew, listen! It's only a short distance, son. You're going to have to jump."

He turned to Santapaola.

"Will you help me?" he asked.

"Of course, but young Andrew shouldn't jump. It's too dangerous for him. He could be buried in a pile of what's left of that section of the school."

"How can you know that?"

"Before I moved here from Sicily, I operated a building trades firm. It taught me a great deal, and not just from theory on some architect's drawing board. I can see cracks in the front of the wall just below the window. Even you cannot know what this means. I see other indications too. *Paisan,* I have pulled myself up from the streets. There are things you learn, practical things. Trust me on this, please!"

Andrew had already climbed up on the narrow window ledge, ready to do as his father had asked.

"What happens if my son jumps now?"

"It may collapse *under* him, and he will surely die if this happens."

Andrew was waiting, terrified, but willing to put himself entirely in his father's hands.

Whatever I ask of him, he will do, Bartlett thought. *That's how I raised him. And now I have the responsibility to . . .*

Andrew was gathering his legs together to make the jump.

"Look!" Santapaola begged, pointing. "The crack is spreading, widening. Your son is young, with not many pounds, but the whole building has been greatly weakened. When the boy jumps, he will be directing pressure against something that may not be able to hold together. Don't risk it, Stephen!"

"All right, all right . . . ," Bartlett acquiesced.

His muscular shoulders sank as he called out to Andrew, "Don't jump just yet, son. Stay where you are."

The boy nodded, though he wasn't sure why his father wanted him to do this.

Both men could hear that part of the building groan, a sound eerily like some giant beast in its death throes.

"He is poised like a feather on the edge of an abyss," Santapaola said. "The slightest breeze will send him over. He must not move now at all, Stephen, not even to climb off the ledge. He must stay as still as his fear will let him."

But Andrew was becoming agitated because of the delay, feeling tremors all through the building.

"Dad, Dad, what should I do now?" he called.

"What does it look like in there?" Bartlett shouted back, trying to steer Andrew's attention elsewhere.

"There's a hallway," the boy replied, glancing behind him, "and stairs on the other side."

"Has anything collapsed where you are? Can you tell, son?"

"I think everything looks all right. Lots of stuff on the floor— plaster, dirt, glass. Some lockers have been flipped over. But the walls and the ceiling are okay."

"We're coming up."

He turned to Santapaola, and sighed as he remarked, "After I left Europe and returned home with my family, I assumed we would be safe. Now, just when I think we are free of the Nazis, they try to draw us right back into their net."

He had doubled his large hands into fists and pulled them slowly toward his body to show his frustration.

As they were heading for a door in that side of the school building, the ground started to rumble under them.

"The foundation is giving way!" Santapaola yelled. "Step back! Hurry!"

They backed up into the street and watched as half of the wall crumbled like a sandcastle at high tide, scattering debris they avoided by dropping to their stomachs and folding their arms in front of their faces.

Bartlett could hear his son screaming in terror.

After a moment, he raised his head slightly—and saw a building that looked little different from one that had been bombed in Berlin or Dresden or another German city, one part of it a heap of fragments, desks, chairs, and blackboards along with concrete and wood and exposed pipes and wires.

That's what this is really all about, he thought. *When every other strategic decision is put aside, this is it! Pure vengeance! They want to inflict some of the same pain and destruction here that we have caused them in their own homeland!*

Andrew was now hanging from what was left of the heavy window frame still attached to the side of the wall that remained standing, though it was unlikely to remain stationary very much longer.

"Let him fall between us," Santapaola said. "We stand below him, Stephen. We catch the boy when he drops."

They hurried up to the wall and linked their hands.

"Now, Andrew!" Bartlett shouted up to him. "We'll save you!"

The pavement trembled.

"He mustn't hesitate," Santapaola said. "We don't have much time."

The nine-year-old, whispering something, let go of the outjutting section of wood. He landed safely in their arms. After being set down on the pavement, Andrew threw his arms around his father's waist and hugged him.

"Thank God you have a son who can do that," Santapaola said wistfully. "I came here from a meeting to plan my own boy's funeral!"

"Can he wait in one of your cars?" Bartlett asked.

"My pleasure, of course."

Andrew looked at him.

"Your son's dead, sir?" he asked.

Santapaola nodded as he placed his hands on the boy's shoulders.

"He was shot by the very evil people who did this to your school," he said..

"Are you going to go after them?"

Santapaola glanced at Stephen Bartlett as he replied, "I would hope that the federal authorities can do that job."

"If they don't?" Andrew pressed, showing a child's tenacity.

"We'll have to see."

Santapaola took Andrew's hand and led him to one of the limousines, then opened the right rear door for him.

As he was returning, one of his men came running up to him. "It's the craziest thing," he said, out of breath. "Some of those people in the crowd are yelling at us to *leave!* Can you believe that? They've recognize you, sir, from newspaper photos and newsreels. They're saying that we have no right to be here, that they want nothing to do with hoodlums.

"They're demanding that we step aside so they can go into the school building and search for their children. They're saying they don't want criminals coming within ten feet of those kids. The rest have no problem, but that handful of troublemakers are trying to disrupt everything."

"Is it what they think of us?" Santapaola asked. "Or is it that we are Italian?"

The other man nodded reluctantly.

"I think you're right, sir!" he exclaimed. "Some were calling us spies for Mussolini!"

Santapaola turned to Bartlett.

"When a man is drowning," he spoke, bewildered, "does it matter if the hand that's extended to him belongs to a criminal or a saint?"

Bartlett had to agree that any such attitude was foolish.

"I'm glad you said that!" Santapaola declared as he turned away from Bartlett and ordered, "Get a Tommy from my limo. With it, you're going to threaten to mow those jerks down as your uncle did to a few hoods at the Saint Valentine's Day Massacre. Tell them if that's the only way you can clear the street, you'll do it. If they think you're bluffing, fire above their heads."

"What then, if they don't budge?"

"Shoot as many as you have to until they get the message!"

The other man ran to one of the limousines, grabbed a key from his pocket, opened the trunk, and came back with a Thompson machine gun.

"Okay, boss?" he asked.

"Go to it," Santapaola said coldly, without blinking.

Bartlett started to protest and go after him, but Santapaola grabbed his arm and pulled him back.

"I can't stand here and let him murder—," Bartlett protested.

"If Francesco is unable to convince that suicidal crowd he's ready to do just that, then there's no way they're going to cooperate—

which they must if more tragedy somehow is to be avoided this day."

Bartlett's expression revealed his loathing for such tactics though he understood that all traffic avenues had to be kept open.

Santapaola's face became red, the veins showing on his forehead.

"Listen to me!" he said, his temper growing along with his impatience. "Yes, I have been what you surely would call a wicked man even from my earliest childhood in Sicily!" he admitted. "But I am not without a feeling heart. I cannot condone the murder of *children!* Or their innocent mothers and fathers!

"That's exactly what has happened already. If we turn our backs on what is going on here, if we do *nothing,* we make matters worse. It becomes a *bigger* victory for the inhumane creatures who are behind all of this!"

He pointed to the screaming, pushing throng just ahead, his men forming a temporary blockade around them.

"The streets *have* to be cleared or it's going to get worse here," he declared, "especially if there are any other explosions and more debris is scattered around. We must do whatever it takes! I've been in the middle of all this before. Already there is a tragedy spread out before us. What *might* happen next will be another, if we allow it to go that far."

Bartlett studied this tough old man: his heavily lined face, thin veins showing on his cheeks, dark circles under eyes that were always bloodshot, thick wrinkled pale lips, nails perfectly manicured, even his "work" clothes handmade and imported, a scent of expensive men's cologne coming from him.

Bartlett was convinced about Santapaola's intentions but still not swayed about his brutal methods.

"I *have* to step in," he spoke. "I have little choice. Don't you see that? I represent the federal government. Under any normal circumstances I would be required to take you and your men into custody. Bodily harm has been threatened against those people, and your men have brandished weapons."

"You disappoint me," Santapaola replied. "Tell me this, will you? Which do you consider to be more important? Arresting me for my *words,* or determining what it is that my *actions* achieve? Answer me that, OK?"

He turned away in disgust and strode toward his men.

"Hey, I've seen that white-haired guy there, the old one, in the newspaper, and not too long ago," someone shouted hoarsely. "He's supposed to be worse than Capone ever was . . . nothing more than a murderer like the rest of them."

Santapaola saw who had spoken, a man in his early forties, clean-shaven, with a closely cropped head of bright red hair.

"All right, mister, do you *really* believe everything you read these days?" he shouted in response.

"No, I don't," the other responded. "But I *do* know all about your kind."

"And what *kind* is that?" asked Santapaola, his tone chilly, his eyes narrowed.

The red-haired individual looked from the old man to the others on either side of him and gulped, suddenly realizing that he was putting himself at great risk.

"I mean, like all of you," he said, "you know, the whole bunch of—"

"*Eye-tal-yans?*" Santapaola growled. "You were going to say something like that, weren't you? Or maybe you had in mind calling us *ginnies*. You think every *dago*—that one's in your vocabulary, too, isn't it?—does what I'm supposed to be guilty of. Tell me I'm wrong, mister, and I *might* believe you!"

He had been portrayed as having the most volcanic temper of all the *Cosa Nostra* chieftains, showing no reluctance to have a man castrated or blinded for some ill-advised comment or behavior, particularly if it seemed to shame his birthright.

He was unaccustomed with moderating his behavior since the power that he had amassed over the years gave him the opportunity to behave in any manner he saw fit.

"Just because of the place of our birth," he spoke deliberately, his tone icy, "something over which *none* of us has any control in life, you believe that *all* of us are involved in crime of some sort. I mean, spit it out, mister. I may *be* a dirty old ginnie—yeah, I may *be* lot of things—but I wager that *you* are starting to smell like a coward."

He interrupted himself, sniffing the air.

"I can detect the stench of a spineless hypocrite who's all words and no action. Where are your guts, mister, when somebody like me stands up to you?"

Another individual raised his voice.

"Wait a minute here! My name's Mainardi," the other man said, stepping out from the crowd. "I'm Italian. I was born and raised in this country. I'm not a gangster. I *hate* what the mafia stands for; I hate how they get their money.

"I'd like to see you come up to *me* right now, whoever you are, and tell me that you think people are criminals just because their families happen to come from Salerno or Sicily or Rome or Florence or some other place in the old country. Go ahead. I'm here. Why don't you tell that to my face, buddy!"

"But all those children?" a young woman with long black hair asked. "I saw you take them away."

"They're waiting in cars a block from here," Santapaola answered. "Look at what's become of the playground, ma'am. They were confused. They were crying or screaming for help or both. None of them knew what to do, with dead bodies everywhere, flames, debris.

"As for myself, I saw what seemed like nothing more than a mob on one side, a plane wreck and a collapsing building on another. I *had* to get those kids out of the way. What would *you* have done?"

The woman gave no response.

"Look!" someone shouted.

Stephen Bartlett had gone to get the youngsters and, like a latter-day Pied Piper, was now leading the line of them up the street.

"They weren't being kidnapped," Bartlett spoke up. "They were sitting in bulletproof cars, sipping soft drinks, and eating pretzels!"

For a moment, no one spoke, not anyone from the crowd or Santapaola and his men or Bartlett. Then one woman spotted her son, and another parent saw his daughter, and someone saw another child and soon most of the parents were hugging most of the children.

Except two little twin boys.

Santapaola saw that they were standing to one side, hugging a telephone pole, and crying. He walked over, bent down beside them, and asked, "Where is your mama? Your papa? Can you tell me that?"

One of them pointed across the street at the playground, then broke down sobbing as he wrapped his arms around Santapaola.

"Under it!" the other shouted. "They're under it!"

"It?" Santapaola asked gently. "The plane, dear child, you mean the plane?"

"Yes!" they both blurted out then.

The old man started sobbing with them.

Someone from the crowd tapped Bartlett on the shoulder. As he turned around, he saw the red-haired individual who had spoken out a short while before.

"My name is Pletcher, Robert Pletcher," he said. "I am very ashamed of myself. What can I do to help?"

"I suggest that you go to the man, Mr. Pletcher. Tell him how you feel. Perhaps that will be enough."

"I would be surprised if it were that simple."

He walked hesitantly over to Santapaola, whose bodyguards were scrutinizing the situation suspiciously until Pletcher stopped and simply stood without speaking a short distance away from the old man, waiting until that moment of intense emotion between him and the twin boys had passed.

"Sir?" he said finally.

As Santapaola stood, anger flashed briefly across his face.

"I feel very badly about what I said," admitted Pletcher. "I feel even worse about what I had been thinking, the kind of attitude that made me so unpleasant, so unfair."

Santapaola seemed pleased.

"It is good that you have done this," he said. "I hold no ill feelings toward you."

He paused, as though listening to some inner voice, cocking his head slightly as he did so.

"I wish I could do something to help," Santapaola remarked then, a wistful tone somewhat softening his normally gruff-sounding voice. "But I know that would be difficult to arrange, given my circumstances. I used to take in homeless children when I was still in Sicily. These two remind me of some of them."

Pletcher was surprised to find himself nodding readily.

"My wife works for the Virginia Child Welfare Agency. She can help finding the right permanent adoptive parents.

Santapaola picked up one of the boys, grunting a bit with the effort.

"I hope you find great happiness," he said. "It would not be difficult for anyone to love you and your brother."

He seemed, for a moment, not a feared mobster but an old man trying to delight a grandchild, and then, feeling his age, he put the boy back down on the pavement.

"I *am* very sorry," he repeated, genuinely humbled.

"If I were honest with myself and with you, young man, I would have to say that I deserve most of the contempt that you have shown. Not everything the newspapers have reported about me can be called lies or distortions, unfortunately."

Suddenly Santapaola's bone-deep weariness seemed almost palpable as he pulled it tightly around himself like a burial shroud.

"I have made this bed of mine and I must be prepared to sleep in it," he added with an air of resignation and a hint of disgust, "though what a pity that my innocent countrymen must suffer derision along with me."

Then Santapaola returned his attention to the twins.

As he was bending down to pick them up the sound of gunfire tore through the air, and a voice shouted, "The next one won't miss, Santapaola. Tell your spaghetti goons to drop their weapons or you die."

19

They've got big cars and machines . . . and . . . and they're threatening a lot of people. There's been a fistfight already."

When Christopher Lyons received a telephone call about some burly mafia-types in a threatening situation, he responded to the anguished female caller by wasting no time assembling a group of other FBI agents. He was convinced she wasn't overreacting or, as was sometimes the case, playing a bizarre prank.

"I don't know what they're doing, but, mister, they've . . . they've got guns, and . . . and I can see what's happening from where I'm standing . . . they're starting to rough up some of the people," stated the shrill, panicky voice. *"Please get here as soon as you can!"*

Less than five minutes earlier, Lyons had been tipped off about the plane crashing into the school and he was ready to leave his office when that second message came through, the caller so completely terrified and loud that he had had to hold the receiver away from his ear.

"We're leaving right now, ma'am," he finally reassured her. "Rest easy. We'll take care of everything."

"God bless you," whoever it was told him.

Before breaking the connection, Lyons thanked her for alerting the FBI, then rang through to the necessary extensions within the bureau, getting together as many men as he could on short notice. Normally Hoover himself would have been notified, but Lyons's perception was that there just wasn't time to locate the director. Thus he took a clear chance of incurring the wrath of a man who knew how to punish a subordinate.

Lyons raced down two flights of stairs and out a side door to the auditorium where nearly two dozen FBI agents, each one heavily armed, were waiting for him. For many years, it had been the designated spot, partly due to its size, for any emergency meetings.

"Some *wops* are trying to muscle in on people after that plane crash," he told them, his belligerency out in the open. "One way or the other, we're needed at the site as soon as we can make it there."

Each man knew about Hoover's dictum against such racist remarks, but since he had broken it himself on several occasions, it had become probably the only one of his many orders that nobody took very seriously anymore.

"I don't know what those guys hope to accomplish, but we can't let them get away with it," Lyons added. "Be prepared for a possible battle, one that *I* have been looking forward to for a long time."

All but one of the men shouted a common readiness. Everyone turned in the sole protester's direction.

"We're not supposed to confront any of the mafioso." The agent, a relative newcomer, spoke up haltingly, tension draining his face of color.

"Use your head, Jenkins!" Lyons interrupted him. "We've got to protect the laws of this nation and, at the same time, innocent people, don't we? I mean, what else are we here for? Think about that, will you?"

Without further protest, the agent nodded, suddenly very sorry that he had ever opened his mouth.

"Follow me!" Lyons yelled back to the drivers of the four other cars that had been made available.

He jumped in behind the wheel of the lead car, and three other agents joined him, two of them sitting in the back. Tires squealed as he raced the Plymouth out of the parking garage under the FBI Building.

In minutes the caravan of black Plymouths and Dodges had crossed over from metropolitan Washington, D.C., into the nearby suburban area, which was not nearly so built-up in those days as it was to become later. They headed toward the plane crash site as well as the place where the gangland-style confrontation had been reported.

Lyons felt invigorated. He was in charge. Hoover happened to be nowhere around. Nor was Stephen Bartlett, for that matter. And they were heading for what might be a violent encounter with the very sort of men he had learned to hate, the kind his father had died fighting years before.

Few of his fellow agents knew of the reasons for his loathing. To them, he often came across as someone who held maniacal racist views about Italians, but he was a top-flight agent and no one bothered to find out why he felt as he did.

There were still times when he would awaken in the middle of the night, imagining that he heard his father's screams in the darkness.

An anonymous witness said he held out for as long as he could, Lyons remembered, *not wanting to give them the satisfaction of hearing his cries of pain. Finally, after beating him, they poured concrete over his body, let it harden, and then dumped him into a reservoir. It took his fellow FBI agents a long time to chip away what the mobsters called a concrete overcoat.*

He gripped the steering wheel tightly.

This time I'll have a chance to put some of them in jail or in graves, as they deserve, he told himself.

"There! All that smoke!" the agent sitting behind Lyons interrupted his thoughts.

Ahead, coming from what could only have been a raging conflagration, a large column of black smoke bellowed up above electrical and telephone lines and the roofs of nearby office buildings and residences.

"Kip, you gotta call every fire department you can think of, and do it right away, buddy," Lyons ordered. "I'm going to concentrate on driving. We might be running a gauntlet the closer we get."

The other agent in the front seat, Kip Gessner, who had joined the FBI soon after Hoover assumed control, cleared his throat as he grabbed for the microphone. "I retire next week, you know. I could be home right now, enjoying a drink with my wife, maybe even a little intimate recreation, yeah, that's right, even at my age. There might be snow on the roof, but I'll guarantee a fire's still burning underneath!" Gessner said.

He chuckled at that familiar line as he took out a small gray notebook from his inside coat pocket and started to look up the fire department numbers, but he never made it past the second page.

"Look out, Kip!" he heard Lyons scream urgently.

The pilot of a small private plane, its instruments performing erratically, had tried to avoid entering the suffocating column of smoke. He did manage to narrowly steer the craft away from the smoke but hurtled into a nearby water tower, which only the day before had been freshly painted a shiny silver. The impact knocked the mammoth structure off its foundation and sent thousands of gallons of water into streets, sweeping over cars, smashing first-floor windows, ripping fragile screen doors off their hinges, and battering other, stronger doors open.

The little plane had exploded on impact, scattering bits and pieces of itself over a wide area; one of the propeller blades that had been sheared off now crashed through the windshield of the first FBI car and straight into the heart of old-timer Kip Gessner, who never got a chance to say good-bye.

Christopher Lyons had frantically tried to avoid the long, thick projectile by swerving the car sharply to the left, but he couldn't do so in time. As Gessner cried out just once, the Dodge skipped over a high curb and crashed into some already dented and rusty garbage cans. Three of the cans were knocked aside, but the fourth wedged under the vehicle, creating sparks on the sidewalk for an instant as momentum kept the car going across what had been a neatly maintained lawn and flower bed. The car lurched up to and over an open brick-faced porch, stopping not more than a foot short of the glass-paned front door of a yellow split-level home with brown wood borders that looked faintly Dutch in their design.

Nor could any of the other cars be stopped in time to avoid fatal collisions since they also had been driven at top speed after leaving FBI headquarters. The third vehicle hit the back of the one in front, was jolted up and over it. The impact flung the Plymouth through midair like an unwieldy boat swept forward on an invisible wave. It landed on the front lawn of a brick-fronted bungalow, then slid over the soft, wet grass, took a chunk out of the right corner of that structure, then skidded through a hedge and collided with the house next door, smashing in the entire left side and collapsing part of the roof as well.

Another car slammed into a telephone pole at the corner, igniting the gas in its tank almost instantly and trapping everyone inside. The remaining car flipped over once, twice, a third time, as the driver veered to one side; it came to rest on its roof, the tires still spinning wildly nearly a minute afterward.

Lyons fell against the steering wheel, losing most of his lunch, his body trembling, groans sputtering from between his cracked lips. Turning his head slowly, mindful of possible muscle and bone damage, he glimpsed Kip Gessner's lifeless body. The propeller blade pinned him to the seat, his head tilted forward, and his chest was carved up like a piece of beef in a slaughterhouse since the sharp projectile had been spinning wildly when it hit him.

The backseat!

Both agents were dead, one of them caught by the end of that blade after it sliced through the front seat. The second man was leaning against the right side, head at an angle, neck twisted and broken by the wrenching impact.

Lyons flung open the door and jumped out.

For a moment he stood in the middle of the torn-up lawn, chunks of grass and dirt strewn about, embedded with fragments of winter-dormant flowers, trying to bring himself under control and ignore the pounding in his head.

Getting his breath and steadying himself, he then dashed on over to each of the three other cars.

Nearly half of the agents were dead, virtually all apparently killed on impact.

They were sprawled across seats or on the floor or had been thrown from a particular car, their bodies on the street or sidewalk or leaning in a sitting position against the trunk of an oak tree.

Of the ones who had survived, only a few were able, on their own, to climb out of their cars. Some doors and windows were blocked by metal that had been twisted around or smashed on top of them.

Someone was screaming.

He looked up at the car that had been flung partway into the side of the house across the street.

"Gasoline!" a familiar voice, muffled, cried out. "I . . . I think it's starting to leak out. Any minute—"

Lyons looked from the vehicle to the house. There must have been people inside—he saw a car parked in the driveway—perhaps an entire family. He knew he had to get them out before he could take care of his fellow agent.

He ran up to the front door and saw that it had been shaken loose from one of its bottom hinges, as though from an earthquake.

Pressing his shoulder against the lacquered plywood, he was able to break it away entirely, he stepped back as it fell with the sound of a bomb blast on a floor littered with chunks of plaster, broken sections of vases, little clay figurines, mirror slivers, overturned furniture, lamps, a few 78-rpm records, and several picture frames.

Dust was thick inside the house.

Lyons started coughing, then wiped his eyes as particles settled in them.

He found the kitchen after stumbling through a rather plushly furnished dining room, noticing the antique grandfather's clock, cut-crystal candleholders, and a large, oval mirror with beveled edges.

And a woman's body on the floor.

A wall cabinet had been shaken loose and was now resting right next to her head, which was surrounded by a puddle of blood.

He bent down, took her pulse, confirmed that she was dead.

Partially blocking a door that he assumed led to the garage was an overturned refrigerator and a large metal table. Since it was too heavy to move, he had to step on top of it and reach his hand down awkwardly to turn the knob on the garage door; he swung the door open as he jumped.

Lyons lost his balance and stumbled, falling only inches from another body, this one a man, on the concrete floor of the garage.

His eyes were open, lifeless.

Lyons stood, noticed that a saw had been wrenched from its spot on the wall, just below the ceiling, where it had dangled on a hook; it had hit the victim on the side of the neck, severing his jugular vein.

Distant cries.

Like the mewing of a cat perhaps.

Lyons stopped breathing for a moment or two, while "hearing" in his imagination the distant tick-tick-ticking of an unseen clock even as the strengthening odor of gasoline reached his nostrils.

Two adults dead, he thought. *Are there children? Am I hearing—?*

He left the kitchen and headed left, down a hallway he assumed led to the bedrooms.

Lyons saw that the ceiling was badly cracked in four places as were the walls, one section of which had pulled away from the studs and protruded a few inches. He found no one in the master bedroom to his right or in the adjoining bathroom.

Behind the next door was a second bedroom, and adjacent to it another bathroom. Both were similarly vacant.

He approached the door at the end of the short hallway.

The sounds! They were coming from inside!

As he placed his hand on the silver knob, he realized the gasoline odor was now much stronger.

Swinging the door open, Lyons saw the front of the Plymouth

wedged in the wall facing him. He started toward it, then, as he glanced toward the opposite wall, noticed a little boy not more than five years old crouched as far into the corner as far he could get, hugging his legs and mumbling incoherently.

Lyons hurried over to him, bent down, wrapped his arms around the child, and started to lift up the thin young body. His own muscles ached and he was glad the boy hadn't proved to be older and heavier; then he turned toward the car as he heard veteran agent Bob Stiernan's weak voice calling to him.

"Forget . . . me . . . ," the other man whispered with painful effort, his cut and bloodied head thrust partway past the twisted window frame on the passenger's side of the Plymouth. "Don't kid yourself, Chris . . . We both know there's not a chance you'll ever get me out of here in time . . . Listen to me! The other guys are piled on top of one another . . . *They're dead* . . . *Monroe, Jameson, Millard, Rayburn* . . . *all of them!*"

The two men heard a spitting, crackling sound.

"Sparks . . . ," Stiernan said. "Hurry, Chris!"

Lyons wavered, tempted briefly to delay taking a stranger to safety rather than turn his back on someone he had known ever since becoming an FBI agent.

"I might be able to—," he started to say.

"Don't, my friend, please don't . . . Something's catching fire . . . I can smell it—*get out of here now!*"

"I'll be back."

Stiernan shook his head.

"You won't . . . ," he said sadly a moment before his voice gave out. "Good . . . luck . . . with . . . Hoover. He's . . . not . . . going . . . to . . . be . . . happy . . . about . . . this."

As Lyons dashed from the room, his eyes were momentarily blinded by a flood of tears and he nearly tripped and fell over an end table that had been tipped on its side. Regaining his balance, he made it to the living room and out the front door before there was an explosion, one that blew apart half the bungalow, showering wood, shingles, pieces of glass, and other materials over him and the little boy.

People were hurrying toward him from their own homes. The surviving agents joined him as well.

A young blonde-haired woman approached and offered to take the frightened and confused child. He thanked her.

"Go, please! Make some phone calls!" he said to the others. "You there! Call the police department. And you, call the nearest fire station. You, next to the telephone pole, call the local hospital. You others, please go down to the corner and stay as far away from here as you can. There might be other explosions."

"Mister!" an elderly man spoke up. "We've all got natural gas here."

As she snapped her fingers, a young woman added, "This whole neighborhood could explode into flames just like that!"

"Make those calls, will you?" Lyons told them, "Listen to the experts when they arrive. Maybe somebody has already called, but you must not take a chance."

He ran back across the street to his car, hoping the trunk's contents hadn't been damaged. The key stuck in the lock for a second or two, then turned. From inside, he grabbed two Tommys and slammed the lid shut.

Several people screamed at the sight of those intimidating weapons, and everyone started to back away.

Resting one Tommy against his leg, he reached into his coat pocket and belatedly pulled out his FBI identification.

"I'm going to have to go now," he said breathlessly after putting his wallet back and grabbing the machine gun. That particular make had achieved an almost celebrity status since it had been used by the celebrated Elliot Ness during his highly publicized raids against the gambling, booze, and prostitution interests of Chicago gangsters including Capone, Frank Nitti, Charles Luciano and others of that era.

"Please!" someone shouted. "You can't just go. You—"

"Harrington School," Lyons asked, ignoring the protest, "can anyone tell me where it is?"

"Yeah . . . six blocks straight ahead. But you've got to—"

Disregarding whatever else was being said, Lyons started to hurry in the direction given.

One of the surviving FBI agents, a younger man named Fred Wallenbach, dashed in front of him.

"Where are you going, Chris?" he asked.

"You know where," Lyons told him. "I can't let those dagos—"

"Listen to me!" Wallenbach pleaded. "My car's radio is working. A message came through. Hoover's personally on the way to that school. He has some men with him. We're supposed to stay here, help out. If any natural gas is ignited, we've got a holocaust on our hands, Chris. You've got to stay."

"I won't stay!" Lyons shouted. "I don't trust Hoover. He's been too friendly with those mobsters."

"I'm no apologist for their kind," Wallenbach spoke, "but I've got to say that without their help, Patton might not have been able to invade Italy as readily as he did. Luciano and his cronies were very useful. And not only there but in *this* country as well. If it weren't for them, more defense and military secrets would have gone to the Nazis, and more buildings would have been blown up."

"You *can't* get into bed with slime and not expect it to rub off on you," Lyons retorted. "They're murderers. I hate them. Every single one should be mowed down *like the animals they are!*"

"Chris, Chris!" Wallenbach begged. "You're a decent man, a brave one, a terrific agent. I love you as a brother. But this thing of yours, this hatred, is going to do more harm to you than it is to any of them. It'll *destroy* you while those you loathe will go right on the way they always have. If you think them so evil, and I agree with you that they are, don't *hand* them this victory, my friend, please don't!"

Images were swirling around in Christopher Lyons's head, images of his father's blood-covered body . . . the years of seeing men like Benedetto Vincenzo Santapaola pile up power as well as millions of dollars in assets, both among the various crime families and also within society in general, even at certain levels of local, state, and national government. Reports of prostitution and pornography rings sprouted up like crabgrass in every state, and all the while, Santapaola, Luciano, Lanski, and the others seemed insulated from the real world, absolved from taking responsibility and retribution for any of their crimes.

"Chris, I . . . I can't let you do this!" Wallenbach said as he started to reach for his Colt, strapped as usual just under his armpit.

Lyons swung the barrel of one of the Tommys across the other man's chin, breaking his jaw. Wallenbach fell to the asphalt, pain making him double up.

"Sorry, Fred," Lyons whispered. "I don't want to do *any* of this. But I have to! You've got to understand that."

Wallenbach looked up at him for a moment, eyes bloodshot, face pale.

Stricken with guilt but now wholly unable to control his actions, Lyons could not face that plaintive stare; he turned away and started to dash up the street.

Scared but curious at the same time, people were looking at him from behind curtains they had pulled aside, letting them drop from their fingers if they thought Lyons caught a glimpse of them.

"I don't care what they're thinking," he muttered, glancing briefly up at the smoke-stained sky. "I've got a job to do. I'm doing it for you, Dad. I'm not going to let you down. I'll take them all with me. *You'll be proud of me!*"

Less than a minute or so later, Lyons could hear some sirens just ahead.

Shortly afterward, an ambulance approached from the opposite direction, and slowed down as the medics spotted him, but he waved them along and it sped on past.

Holding a fully loaded Tommy in each hand with a standard issue Colt strapped to his side, FBI agent Christopher Lyons, perspiration soaking him despite the chill of early November, continued up that second block and into the next as fast as the burden of such heavy firepower would allow him to run.

20

Tell your spaghetti goons to drop their weapons or you die . . . .

Christopher Lyons was standing on a corner at the intersection, the crowd to his left and Bartlett, Santapaola, and the twin boys to his right. He continued to hold a Tommy gun in one hand but had fired over their heads with the Colt he held in the other. The second Tommy lay on the ground near his right leg.

Benedetto Vincenzo Santapaola's men tensed as they waited for a signal from their boss. He hesitated for a second or two, surveying the situation, and decided there wasn't an alternative to obeying the FBI agent. When he gave one quick nod, they slowly put their firearms down on the asphalt street.

"Step away from those kids!" Lyons demanded.

"Christopher . . . ," Bartlett started to protest as he stood next to the old man. "Rest easy, please. It's all right now. Everything's in—"

Lyons laughed harshly at that.

"You really *have* flipped," he shouted sarcastically. "Either that or you've sold out to these criminals. I wouldn't be surprised if both were true."

He gestured with the Tommy.

"Take those boys, Bartlett, and walk slowly away from Santapaola. *Now!*"

Flashing through his mind were images of his father dying as three gunmen opened fire at him. They continued until the body was unrecognizable.

"My father had to be buried in a closed coffin because of men like him," he said, quickly losing any control. "I was too young to understand, at first, what had happened to him. At the funeral I threw a flower onto the lid of the coffin. I was crying and couldn't see what I was doing."

His fingers tightened reflexively on the trigger of each weapon, his face now an overwrought, angry red.

"I stumbled over into the grave itself. Without thinking I grabbed for the coffin to steady myself, and succeeded in knocking it from the straps that were holding it. It fell on top of me, but at the same time the lid sprang open and my father's body, smashed and torn by dozens of bullets, fell out next to me."

He nearly choked as the memory overwhelmed him.

"I saw how little of my father's body was left. I screamed so hard and so long when I saw him that I started to cough up blood over whoever it was who reached down and pulled me out of the grave."

Lyons felt dizzy, his legs wobbly.

"I had to be hospitalized," he went on, his voice unsteady. "No one knew if I would even pull through."

He pointed the Colt directly at Santapaola.

"I clung to one thought—one, yes, compulsion—to wipe out garbage like him, to save as many sons and daughters as possible from going through what I did."

He motioned with the Tommy.

"I'm telling you one last time to step away from that monster!" he yelled.

"Why?" Bartlett demanded, suspecting the answer. "Because you're planning to *murder* him now in front of all these people? And aren't you going to claim that you were just freeing them from possible harm? That means you would be a hero, right, and at the same time be able to satisfy this maniacal loathing of yours?"

"Maniacal?" Lyons spit out the word. "Who's the maniac here? Me? Or you, Bartlett? You're the idiot who wants to protect a man no better than gutter scum more than you want to perform your duty."

"Santapaola could become a different man."

He saw the mobster wince as he said this.

"Bull!" Lyons scoffed. "It's all a facade; you should know that. A week from now, he'll order a gangland execution of someone, *anyone* who dares to cross him. A month after that, it'll be somebody else for yet another reason. He's survived this long because he's clever. How can you ignore *any* of what I'm saying? It's true; you can't deny that."

The problem for Bartlett just then was that Lyons was making some sense.

He glanced at the twins. Whatever happened next, they would have to be kept safe. So he took each by the hand and walked them over to the crowd, picking a young couple standing to the side.

"Will you look after them for a little while?" he asked.

Both responded eagerly.

The screech of tires spun him around. All eyes turned toward the source.

A black sedan had pulled up on the opposite side of the intersection.

The passenger door opened and someone got out who was hardly difficult to recognize.

J. Edgar Hoover.

"A message came to my office less than half an hour ago," he spoke expansively. "I would have been here sooner, but a communications breakdown and clogged roads thwarted me. All the help needed will be here shortly from the various fire and police departments as well as my own office."

He glanced at Christopher Lyons.

"What in the devil are *you* doing, Lyons?" he demanded.

"Please step aside, sir."

"Why in the world are you threatening any of these people instead of pitching in and helping out?"

"The man in back of you, sir, is—"

"I *know* who he is, Lyons," interrupted Hoover. "Now put your weapon away and let's get to business."

"Santapaola has a long criminal record, sir. He was strong-arming these good people. And I have no idea what he was planning to do with those boys."

"Nonsense!" Robert Pletcher spoke up. "I admit we all thought that at first. But the opposite was true then and now: These men were only trying to help us, Mr. Hoover."

"If that is the case, tell me why, Mr. Santapaola, will you please?" the director asked, his voice more conciliatory than suspicious or demanding.

Santapaola stepped forward.

"I do *not* harm children, nor do I *allow* them to *be* harmed if I can prevent that from happening," he said. "I was trying to see that they were cared for while this man's wife seeks a suitable adoptive couple."

"Liar!" shouted Lyons. "What about the children of men you have killed? How many go to sleep fatherless each night because of you?"

Before Santapaola could answer, half a dozen other cars pulled up along one of the other streets leading into the intersection, FBI agents jumping out of each.

Hoover walked up to Lyons.

"Hand me those weapons, Christopher," he spoke, not noticing the other Tommy on the ground. "We'll try to help you. I know some of the details about your father. I *can* understand how much of a nightmare you must have faced."

Hoover lowered his voice to a whisper, gentle, kind.

"Will you do this, please?" he asked. "I will personally take care of everything, son. Just give me the Colt and the Tommy; that's all I ask."

"You call me son after *this,* sir?"

"Yes, I know your record. I will not crucify you. You are a good and decent man."

Lyons started sobbing as he thrust the two weapons out before him and Hoover took them gently from his grasp.

The FBI director turned and shouted to the other agents to reholster their own guns, which they had drawn in the meantime.

People in the crowd were audibly sighing with relief a moment before Christopher Lyons abruptly pushed Hoover to one side and retrieved the remaining Tommy, lifting it up and pointing it toward Santapaola.

In an instant the mobster's gunmen had gotten their own weapons and opened fire on Lyons, but not before he fired off a round of shots.

Seeing what was happening, Robert Pletcher dashed in front of Santapaola and took the machine-gun barrage himself. He was flung backward against the old man by the force of the bullets.

Santapaola was nearly knocked off his feet by the impact of a 160-pound man but somehow managed to remain standing, his arms wrapped tightly around Pletcher, the other man's blood quickly soaking him.

He glanced at Bartlett, who had run up to the two of them.

"This man gave his life for me, Stephen," he said, puzzled, stunned. *"Why did he do that? Why did he do that?"*

"Let me help you," Bartlett offered.

"*No!* I will do this myself!"

He bent down with the body and laid it on the asphalt, then took off his coat and placed it over Robert Pletcher's chest and head.

"It is a pity," he whispered to Bartlett after he stood with some effort, "that my men have been here to see this."

"Why? I should think they'd feel a great deal of sympathy for you, a great deal of respect."

"Not in my world, Stephen. I have shown what some of them will perceive as weakness. That's how it starts, you know. One or the other will begin plotting against me, calling meetings behind my back in smoke-filled rooms, a paid killer hired to do the job."

He pointed sadly at the body.

"One day not so very long from now, I'm afraid, Stephen, I expect to end up like this poor fellow here."

Benedetto Vincenzo Santapaola pressed his left hand against his chest, then held that hand out, palm up, in front of him as he added, "Only for the moment is that blood not my own."

21

As it turned out, damage was mainly confined to the Harrington school property itself and a handful of homes across the street from it, as well as that single residence on the route taken earlier by Christopher Lyons and the other FBI agents. No other neighborhoods were involved. That which had been feared—a gas-main blowup and a resulting conflagration—did not occur.

There were a few uneasy moments between Santapaola's gunmen and the agents who had witnessed one of their own being killed by gangsters. But, however the two groups ordinarily would have reacted, both seemed to understand that the present situation was a different one altogether, that Lyons had gone berserk, and the important thing became preventing *him* from shooting anyone, for, in his unbalanced state, he might not have stopped at Santapaola. Even so, an innocent man died, and this was not a time for any macho displays of retaliation.

J. Edgar Hoover offered again to take Bartlett home. Bone-tired, muscles sore, head aching, the OSS agent gratefully accepted.

The drive was spent mostly in silence until, a short distance away, Hoover had the driver stop the car at the curb next to a large vacant lot. He got out, Bartlett following him.

Hoover breathed in deeply.

"The air is clear here," he said. "Perhaps there will come a day when we will not be able to enjoy this privilege so easily."

He reached into his coat pocket and took out a teletype message that had been sent to him from William Casey's office.

"*Bloody Winter* has been canceled!" Bartlett exclaimed as he read its contents. "A list of all locations where sabotage preparations have been completed will be sent in a matter of hours. No others are to be attempted. In fact, all agents previously associated with *Bloody Winter* have been recalled."

"That was the first message," Hoover stated. "A second was comprised of that very list, an immensely useful one, of course."

"Sir?" Bartlett asked.

"Yes, Stephen?"

"There was another message, wasn't there?"

Hoover smiled with appreciation as he admitted, "There was. Here it is."

He retrieved the second sheet from the same pocket as the first.

"Unbelievable!" Bartlett exclaimed once he realized the staggering revelation that was printed on it.

"I very much agree with that assessment. But what you have just learned *is* quite true. Casey assures me that the information has been checked out thoroughly."

"Not just a ploy of some sort?"

"Precisely."

They had been leaning against Hoover's car as the two of them talked. Bartlett slid down to a sitting position on the street, his back against the right fender.

"Are you all right, Stephen?" asked a genuinely concerned Hoover.

"Oh, I am, sir; I am! Thank you for asking. I was just struck by how, even in the most vile individuals, some little decency, some little remnant of leftover good, sometimes seems to spring back to life after being buried for most of a lifetime."

Hoover did something out of character then by sitting down next to him, their shoulders touching.

"My men think me aloof, sometimes cold and cruel," he acknowledged. "I mustn't spoil the illusion, you know. This sort of thing is necessary, I feel, for the kind of discipline I have always considered inescapable. You understand my meaning, I trust."

What Hoover meant was that that little moment should remain a private one between the two of them.

"I do, sir, completely," Bartlett told him as he returned that sheet of paper.

"By order of Heinrich Himmler . . . ," said Hoover. "After months of planning, staggering expense, imprisonment of some of his top operatives, he throws it all out the window. Undoubtedly he wants to save face when the Allies emerge victorious from the war."

"His face and his butt, I imagine!" Bartlett said.

"But there must be more to it than that, Stephen. What about those contacts of his last year with the International Red Cross some few weeks before the truly hopeless course of the war had become quite so glaringly obvious, even to the *Führer*'s deluded henchmen?

"And just recently, Hitler demanded that all the extermination camps be leveled and the bodies of prisoners be disposed of as quickly as possible. Himmler went ahead and secretly countermanded any such orders. In fact, he has begun slipping Jews out the back door of some of the camps, men, women, and children in less dire physical condition than many of the others, apparently because they present a less grisly image to the outside world—you know, best foot forward and all of that."

"I have heard that, presumably after his scheme for deposing Hitler succeeds," Bartlett interjected, "Himmler hopes to lead the Fatherland in an alliance with the Allies against a common enemy that he is predicting could precipitate a worldwide obsession for the next half a century or more, if not contained."

"The Communists?"

Bartlett, smiling, nodded at that.

"Himmler now has been claiming that *their* crimes eventually will make the Nazis look like choirboys, that a hundred million lives will be lost," he said. "It will be interesting to see if he is only babbling or there is some factual basis to what he says."

"I suppose we had better get you back home now," Hoover said, sighing. "A simple phone call reassuring your wife isn't enough, under the circumstances."

"Did you have something else that you wanted to mention, sir?"

Hoover looked at him, not quite knowing what to make of someone for whom his respect was growing dramatically.

"I didn't know that reading someone else's mind was another Christian gift of the Spirit," he said, "at least twice in just a few minutes."

"It isn't. You seem as though—"

Hoover unexpectedly averted his eyes from Bartlett.

"I would be happy to listen, sir," Bartlett assured him.

"An irony, Stephen, just an irony."

Bartlett waited for Hoover to tell him what it was.

"I was just thinking that it is not so unlikely, you know, that some of my worst political enemies are capable of rewriting the truth and thereby turning Heinrich Himmler into a hero should that man somehow get his wish about becoming his country's next leader. And at the same time, they could step up their insidious campaign of denigration by continuing to portray me as some kind of egotistical devil who should be in jail himself!"

As he faced Bartlett again, Hoover's expression was one of profound sorrow and regret.

"Can it perhaps be, Stephen, that history, however unfairly, will judge me more harshly than one of the chief architects of genocide?"

He bowed his head for a moment, struck by a thought that was both ludicrous and chilling at the same time.

"I don't know that I could bear that," J. Edgar Hoover spoke, barely above a whisper. "I don't know that I could at all."

Though Bartlett had finally reached home, he was not yet alone with his wife Natalie and his son Andrew. After waving good-bye to Hoover and entering the house, he saw a familiar figure sitting on the living-room sofa.

William Casey.

"Your wife has been a wonderful hostess, Stephen," he said, a strange joylessness in his manner as he stood.

He turned to Natalie.

"I'm very glad your son wasn't seriously hurt," he told her. "But he must be a very tired young man right now."

Andrew had been brought home by an FBI agent after being examined by medics. Following a few moments of hugging his mother and eating a quick sandwich, with a glass of milk, the nine-year-old went straight to his bedroom, and fell asleep easily.

"I'll go upstairs now," she said, "and see how he's making out."

Natalie put her arms around her husband and the two of them kissed briefly, then after smiling pleasantly at Casey, she walked upstairs.

"What brings you here, sir?" Bartlett asked cautiously.

"It's not over, Stephen," replied Casey. "In some respects, it won't *be* over for decades."

Bartlett had no idea what his boss was talking about and said so.

"The paint," Casey went on, "the bloody paint!"

At the mention of that, Bartlett's palms turned sweaty.

Back at the airfield . . .

"What about the paint, sir?" he asked, his throat dry.

"We have the list provided by Himmler and we've taken steps to scour the locations mentioned. It will be quite a job but we can do it."

"And yet there is still a problem?"

Casey looked up at the ceiling.

"Oh, Stephen, yes, there is still a problem. That paint—"

"At the airfield, sir?"

Several very large canisters of silver paint . . .

Still looking upward, Casey replied, "That's right. Nobody then had any idea what it entailed. In an era of wartime budgetary caps, it seemed harmless enough to use some of the enemy's own supplies.

"The paint, and there was a great deal of it, was simply divided up and transferred to the department of highways and to other agencies. Certain members of Congress got some cans. But we can trace the supply only part of the way."

He looked at Bartlett now.

"The rest is just gone, swallowed up by our bureaucracy. It's out there somewhere, being used by innocent people for innocent purposes."

Isn't that crazy? What's so special about paint of any color? We saw some of those guys pouring it from one of the canisters into what looked like ordinary paint cans. What are we to make of that? It seems so pointless . . .

Bartlett felt the muscles in his throat constricting.

"It could be used anywhere . . . ," he muttered.

"At airports, at other schools, at an endless, unknown variety of places, Stephen."

Casey's right hand had begun to twitch in visible spasms. He grabbed it with his other hand and held it until it was calm again.

"I hate to parade out a cliché but something does need to be said if we are to be honest, and here goes, Stephen: Now implanted within the very structure of this nation are time bombs of a sort, ready to go off."

Tiny transistors, primitive little creations . . .

"Some will fail after awhile, of course," Casey continued. "Others will be defective and nonoperational from the outset."

"But the rest, sir—what about the rest?"

"That's right, Stephen. Year after year we'll have to wonder. Communications are scrambled. Planes crash without apparent reason. There are explosions at oil refineries. On and on it goes. We'll never know when the danger has finally passed. It may not be in my lifetime or yours."

Even in the most vile individuals, some little decency, some little remnant of leftover good, sometimes seems to spring back to life after being buried for most of a lifetime.

Stephen Bartlett had a mental image then of Heinrich Himmler, in the midst of anguish eternal, laughing for a brief and terrible moment before a thousand grasping demons pulled him back once again into the always-consuming flames of hell itself.

The final solution.

Epilogue

Thirty years later, at Chicago's O'Hare Airport, an American Airlines passenger jet crashed seconds after takeoff . . .

Finis